NIGHT FALLS, SUN RISES

A Continuum of Tales
and
Short Stories

by
Dedwydd Jones

For Karl Francais
Happy Memories!
Hwyl fawr,
Dedwydd.

CONTENTS AND ACKNOWLEDGEMENTS

For my dearest daughters Caryl, Awen and Caroline my deepest thanks for keeping the dream going.

I would like to thank Mr Maruti Morajkar in particular for his invaluable help and advice in the difficult matter of computers and their peculiar ops.

"And death shall be chosen rather than life by all the residue of them that remain of this evil family." **Jeremiah 8,3**

"How to keep-is there ány any, is there none such, nowhere known some, bow or brooch or braid or brace, lace, latch or catch or key to Keep Back beauty, to keep it, beauty, beauty, beauty…from vanishing away?

No there's none, there's none, O no there's none…
Be beginning to despair, to despair,
Despair, despair, despair, despair…"
The Leaden Echo, Maidens' song, **by Gerard Manley Hopkins**

NIGHT FALLS, SUN RISES
a continuum of tales

In a violent storm, **the 5.50 Express** to Terminus Geneva sped along the scenic lakeside route. After a ear-splitting clap of thunder directly overhead, Nickador's formerly silent, solitary companion had, strangely, begun making faces, gazing fixedly at his own smudged reflections in the window of the compartment. The deluge outside was illuminated by flashes of sheet lightning, which, at first, didn't seem to upset the man too much. Each image of the man's face was distorted by the droplets smashing against the glass outside and made his features appear bloated, mongoloid even, as in a nightmare. The man rapidly switched expressions – disbelief first, then outrage, grief, his eyes sometimes screwed shut, his throat full of alarming growls; hatred followed by love, guilt by innocence, and finally the total tearful resignation of a confessed sinner, mea culpa, hands clasped. The man now abruptly terminated his facial exercises as if he had run out of emotions. He suddenly peered outside into the darkness and waved as to a waiting friend, "Hi there!" he shouted, but Nickador realised the man was not addressing his own image this time but someone else's. "Hey you, Simon out there, look at me when I'm talking to you!" He turned to Nickador, "My son, Simon, you know, was swept off the bows of the yacht in just such a storm as this when I was at the tiller, and he drowned like a rat. I was a beginner. I was no good. His body was never recovered. Hey!" he shouted, waving and beckoning, "Is it you out there Simon, stirring up the storm? Is it you who sent those winds to blow away all my washing in the garden yesterday and make me feel so awful?" He cocked his ear at the howling gusts of wind and stared at the floods of rain. "Hey you, Simon, it's not true, what they say… I wasn't at the wheel…I…"

The man slumped down on the seat, clasped his arms round his knees and began rocking to and fro, sobbing uncontrollably. The storm rolled on outside, increasing in fury as they approached the final stop. It seemed to envelope the compartment, the carriage, the whole train, indeed, their very existence. The faces of the dear drowned faded on and off, ancient, fresh multitudes of headshot, heart-torn victims of some Super Nova shit-bang, us, I have a passion for echoes…some time or other… let me nod off, svp… Zzzz…Zzzz…Zzz…Go! Go! Go! Up! Ha, ha, ha! Somebody. Yelling…In a trice, Nickador was alert, listening, seeing…his **Ma-in-Law and Karen**, her daughter, his wife, having their hundredth spiteful spat of the week. He was now crouched down in the Concierge's broom-cupboard by the main entrance to Ma's luxury, apartment, the very acne of bourgeois comfort and respectability. His hidey-hole no one looked into, a place where only rubbish was deposited and cleaning fluids filled the stinky shelves. The remorseless, discordant recriminations were, as usual, disclosing the murky, familiar, waters which no one should have disturbed. He sighed. He'd really dropped himself into it this time! Why? Oh, why, what a twit, no chicken like an old chicken…the clouds billowed overhead… they threatened to suffocate him, all to no avail…they reverberated again and Karen now in the corridor close to his little den, hammered on the apartment door. She paused in her thumpings and pulled out her buzzing mobile. A voice crackled over. It was her mother, on the inside, determined to reciprocate her daughter's recent 'insults' to her. Ma's voice could be heard through the door, a mine of vicious information.

"Karen?! You there! What do you want now?!"

"Ma, you've locked the door again. I can't get in."

"I haven't got a spare key."

"You're throwing me out!"

"No, I'm not."

"Where am I going to live?"

"I can't give you any more money."

"I'll get some from Pa when he dies!"

"So will I – when he dies. Everyone knows what

you're after. "

"If I visited the clinic, it was to give Pa flowers, honey drops for his chest…

"…you and your stupid 'body balms…'pots of azaleas, apricots…god knows what!"

"…he was gasping, breathless…"

"…he was unconscious…"

"…he was turning pink. Doctor Klein gave him chloral hydrate."

"What's that?!"

"It always helps, like Bromo Selzer, he said. Now let me in!"

Karin hammered on the door. She finally stopped, helpless. "See!" she heard her mother laugh in triumph, "violence will get you nowhere. This is my home, and it stays mine!"

"But we can't talk like this, the neighbours…"

"…you're just interfering again, that's what the doctor said."

"No, Ma! He's my Pa," Karen half-whispered.

"Doctor Klein is the director of the Clinic. He's the man who made sure every last penny of Pa's Charity money went into the new wing. That donation was to thank Dr Klein for last summer…Pa wouldn't be here except for him…the by-pass…"

"…after which dangerous operation Pa hid in the hospital toilet for a 'secret' smoke…"

"…Doctor Klein knows Pa inside out, like I know you, and I don't believe a word you say."

"I did not visit Pa yesterday!"

"Doctor said you visit him nearly every night."

"The doctor is a liar!"

"Hark at you, Miss Brazen! He said you only see your poor Pa when he's alone."

"There was always a nurse present, Dr Klein's Head Nurse - that was the arrangement. Pa insisted on it."

"He didn't trust any of you, that's why he gave that money to Dr Klein. Pa might go at any time, especially after his seizure at the bar-b-q, he still smokes, such a let down…still not over it…"

"…then there's our deep cover…"

"Keeping it up like this , are you?"

"Dear Dr Klein might get the lot."

"Nonsense! His fair share, for charity's sake, what Pa says."

"There's no Will that I know of, and I am next of kin."

"I'm seeing Pa this afternoon."

"And don't take your 'Nickador' with you, he's not one of the family. You and your stupid, shameful … wedding, that stupid name, 'Nickador'!…"

"…why did Pa give all that money to Dr Klein?"

"To show you lot where he stood, doing the right thing…"

"A moral gesture? That's a joke. Tax deduction more like."

"You're a fine one to talk. I mean, the scandals, this Nickador 'marriage,' what people think! Remember nasty aunty Harriet, as if she didn't have enough trouble with her half-dead hubby Maurice and her own perverted kids, what did she see in the Royal Hotel, the best hotel in town, it would be her, everyone who was anyone went there, on the wall of the ladies' toilet all those years ago, dare you remember? Let me refresh your memory - 'If you want a good… 'shag'… ring Julie!' Your sister!... "at…" and the number was of here, my apartment, my home! and your name added under hers… "

"…that was just out of spite, to add my name, Julie did that."

"That story's still doing the rounds. And worse. And that 'boy friend' of hers, a dishcloth if there ever was one, grows pot under the sunflowers in his garden, and goes to church every Sunday to sell the product. A mafia! And your own 'Nickador,' what a chump. Why doesn't he change his stupid name? Never a word, skulks in corners, he'll never get a job here. Got to get up and go, go go…as Pa says…!"

"…Nickador is a qualified teacher."

"Why does he poke his nose in here, Pa and all?"

"He just drives me to the Clinic…"

"…in my car"…

"…that rattle-trap…"

"…just because Pa won't buy me a new one…"

"…danger of death…thank god"

"Never! Those slanders have got to stop! We are not conspiring anything, any of us, the immediate family holds its head up high. So we've got a reserve plan, so what. Normal. As for Julie's 'dishcloth,' a gangster, I tell you!"

"Well, don't accuse me of having anything to do with it! And keep your voice down!"

"You got a certificate in Pharmacy studies or something, so use it. You live on that weed."

"No, we don't."

"Liars, both of you, so don't come the high horse with me!"

"You've got enough money for the rest of your life."

"No, I haven't!"

"And more for the next!"

"Ha, ha, ha! Did he say anything?"

"Who?"

"Your Pa of course, he's still boss."

"He's unconscious most of the time, as you've said enough times."

"And let me tell you, your Grandpa would've taken the strap to you and your sister before kicking you out!"

"Rubbish! Grandpa was a …."

" …just to remind you, I am the legal heir to everything. Doctor Klein said Pa was on the brink, and that your visits 'did little to help him'."

"Just more lies that you make up as you go along."

"You know what I mean, and so does Pa and the Doctor! I don't want you in my home any longer… true or false!..."

"…what about the spare room?"

"For storage, you know that."

"I'll visit Pa when I like."

"You've found the Will then?"

"You've hidden it somewhere."

"Ask your Pa again, he knows where it is."

"I am not going to give in."

"Well, don't come back here."

"It's…. just…. about… Xmas…"

The clouds lift…to …who's next in the grisly fly past? The images flit like midges at sunset, faint, luminous and clinging, like last year's lot. A true plague never stops, and why should it? Heart's just one big, bruised, weeping sponge, fading now over the lochs and Minervian promontories to the sound of pibrochs diminishing … Jesu!... not harps now?!…but…but… but…why not try sheer beauty, the evening sky, en rose, for example, before the bars and shutters go up...or down…whichever the case may be...Zzzz…Zzz…Brrr… brrr…He snatched up his mobile. **Dear Dr Ash,** you again! What's that?" Faintly, he made out - "Wake Up! Wakey, wakey!" Nickador shook himself. Ash's voice was crisp and clear. "There! See, Nickador, the glints and gleams of Manorbier, faster than ancient light itself!" "Thank god for you, Dr Ash, old mate bass guitarist, and older physician, you listen too. The tale of the picture went thus:

"Midnight and the tide was on the turn. Nickador and Karen stood on the edge of the foaming moon-surge creeping towards them. A myriad reflections sparkled around the endless foamy little wavelets. They saw the horizon misting up and the black clouds billowing towards the shore. The huge turreted castle of Manorbier, built on vast ancient upsurges of volcanic granite, stood like a hunched giant before the mainland. The moon slipped momentarily out of its vast aerial shadowy cavern and illuminated the whole scene. The little island jutted out sea-ward, its beetling, tumbled heights thrusting irresistibly upwards and on the lower slopes of the interior ward of the bastion, a three-hundred and twenty-yard outer curtain-wall ran alongside the long-emptied moat, with its ruined terraces, dismantled granaries and looted treasures, the castle gardens long laid waste. Scorch marks disfigured the yellow blocks of ashlar stone along the base line. The vast drum-towers of the edifice above streamed with the flags and pennants of the Lord of the Demesne of Manorbier, the Count of Denzel. Him and his thousand intricate carved crestings in the great Hall! - solid crap out of the College of Heralds, thought Nickador…. 'pride goeth…!' He started as he swore he briefly saw the ghost called the White Lady hovering at the entrance to the Treasury Turret. He shook off the feeling, for it was bound to be only that. A flying archway curved over the Gatehouse entrance, the suspended polished steel points of the double-portcullis still gleaming in the invading dark; arrow loops, multiple cross-bow slits, spy holes for the molten lead, and elevated walk-ways ran along the huge cruel face of the front of the formidable fortress, which seemed to take on the shape of a screaming skull. As he stood there with the tide lapping about his feet, he, the Knight Nickador, swore he could hear the clash of arms and the sound of ignorant armies slashing each other at night - while above, from every pinnacle and flag-pole streamed the victorious arms of the merciless Lord Denzel. Nickador stared harder into the gathering gloom. The shifting surges of dark clouds seemed to envelope him. Above the screams and yells of the battle cries, a flock of cawing, carrion crows swooped down on the quest for bloodier pickings and richer meat, all littered about him. What a vision!

Nickador had deliberately brought his splendid, new, independent twenty-two year old wife, Karen, blond, short, brown eyed which seemed at first to be ducking all questions of nice or nasty, what a falling off! - here to this magical spot at midnight so she could behold and feel the silvery splendour of the place. He noticed the tide creeping in over her strap-on, golden sandals. She spoke without facing him.

"Don't you wish you were looking at this with somebody else?"

Her echoing voice sounded more than ever like a predator bird of the air hovering over its prey, before soaring away into the glorious heavens of argent and gold – thank God for someone to thank…I think… forever dozey…never to be touched really…by any tide incoming or out…I hoped…we hoped, he/she/it/ hoped and hoped and found none except that which still lives, they say, in the secret, scarred, and scarlet spaces of the drop't guillotine ... whoosh! – help! or something like that, all around in heavy fog...my reveries so concrete, vague...Dr Ash, I keep on having ludicrous trains of thought! What to do? Zzzz...Zzzz...Zzz..." Wake up call, man, rise and shine!!" "Not again, Dr Ash!!" "Up, up! Go, go, see the white alp in stony, liquefied turbulence! Go, go on! **The Avalanche, man!"**

On the day after Dr Ash's incessant urgings, Nickador stood on the upper slopes in serene sunlight. Below him lay the massive body of the expired avalanche, an immense beached whale. It had had swept down the steep corridors between the conifers, thundered across the macadamed road, into the car park of the four-storey Mirador hotel, taking thirteen vehicles with it, then leapt over the rim of the parking area and hit the piste rouge – which area had been designated red for danger, and still the avaricious bastards built on it! - two empty chalets were then engulfed, sweeping off the jutting balconies, breaking all the windows up to the third floor. The vast manic bulk then ran out of steam and came to a stop not ten yards from the Mirador hotel's night club entrance. In the high front of the stalled mass, he saw a yellow Mercedes sticking out, as if rammed there by a huge hand. The car body was skewered by the trunk of a splintered pine, in through the boot, out through the roof! - the rear doors torn off, suitcases split open by the impact. The whole area was

scattered with what seemed huge matchsticks, the shards
of the trees swept away on the slope. Breast- stroke your
way out of that!? as the Mirador guides advised?! Not a
hope! The boulders were reinforced by huge slabs of ice,
each one a potential death blow. He paused, feeling all
upside down, like the machines! He could make out
more vehicles trapped in the shiny, monstrous coils of
the snow blast: Fiats, Aston Martins, Volkswagons, god
knows how many more in the depths, a veritable car
cemetery in the drifts! And the hotel guides had
announced afterwards, it was all due to – grass! Spring
had come early and the grass had had plenty of sunlight
and grew prolifically so that it stood high. In the sudden
last snowfall, the grass had been forced flat and
provided, a perfect slidy, platform for the snow to launch
its bulk from – right down to the end of the danger
slope! Why invite catastrophes of nature, when all nature
wants, he suspected, like most people really, is to be left
in peace. A huge ghastly eeriness pervaded the whole
place. He stared around. Yes! It was the silence. Where
were the emergenciy services? It was as if he was
standing in the middle of a huge bubble with no echoes
even from the outside world, thank god. But he had been
spared the Avalanche, nature's wrath, and the Mirador
too, by yards, and all in the middle of this spectral,
immense stillness. Yes, so what? He'd drink to it. Bet Dr
Ash has never seen the like, he muttered - but with the
usual chill of irony. He trudged over to the Hotel
Mirador. The 'Skiing Café' seemed to be closed. He
moved over to the restaurant dining rooms and went

inside. It was vile. The hotel had not been built out of love but out of money. His first quick glance made him shudder. He passed under an arch of plastic vines loaded with fake bunches of grapes, with facsimile models of Ferrari cheese presses on either side. The lobby and dance floor were empty, evacuated no doubt, but he suspected this was due to the foul décor, not the nearness of the threatened disaster a few feet outside. The walls, he saw, were constructed of stacked flints imbedded in cement. They glowed with a sickly yellowish colour – someone had varnished them. These were side by side with bottle tops fixed into the mortar as well, fields of gay poppers with scarcely a glint. Slabs of slate sticking out from the walls acted as tables. The ceiling was divided into ill-fitting orange plasterboard panels, just pasted on with industrial glue. A forest of bottle corks hung down by string from the fake scorched beams bearing fairy lights, now fortunately darkened. Apart from the cheese and wine paraphernalia, there were, to offer a contrast - recently manufactured motor car number plates, oddly all from Richmond, Virginia; imitation antique skis from Davos, made by Donatello, the Italian blacksmith hired for the season; rows of glaring slot machines, now mercifully dimmed; 'honey mead morphemes' behind the bar - work that one out!; another enigmatic notice, 'the mechanism to lower the plates is the screw or the hydraulic device at the base of the barrel;' next to mini-samples of 'Ravensberg,' ' Romanina' and 'Hebrew' concoctions, all without a trace of any kind of human odour, 'de-acidification,' 'de-stemming' and 'piceage' having taken place. The bung closures were inordinately fine and one hundred per cent tight: all appurtenances running with tendrils of creeping plastic vine. He was taken aback by the inverted bed-pan-warmers on the shelves, all full of false stinky dessert camembert, blue slabs crawling with maggots, a realistic touch there! croquet mallets, going back to a more elegant age; baskets of barley and oats, all real and shedding their fruit in thousands onto the unswept floor; tongueless cowbells dangling among the dead bulbs above the bar; half-sawed barrels as seats, with iron-wrought gig-lamps, rusting scythes, sickles by the score in the offing; now to harvest time among the meadows, with garlands of wheat everywhere; oxen heads in yokes of teak; piles of glistening artificial logs by a flaming fire of gas; modern cuckoo clocks dotted around like birds lost in a false mechanical, nightmarish wilderness; wagon-wheels proliferated along the way to the toilets; a brand new ovalmaltine dispenser rose proudly by the rows of schnapps and pommes, obliging the guests, drunk or sober; over all, hanging by a shoelace, was a suspended a mighty boxing glove clenched into a fist about to strike, the legend threatening 'Out for the count! NO CREDIT!' and then! – he hesitated, no, surely this was not real - splayed out on the wall, nailed up meticulously, was a complete wild boar, the furry head m drooping down over its recently scooped out crimson chest – it ponged ferociously - could it be real? He reached out a hand and recoiled with a grunt of disgust, bits of flesh still adhered to the skin.

Barbarians! They had not even had the decency to scrape off the last of the fragments of living boar tissue for him. With a half-heave of the stomach, he turned himself around and strode towards the outside. For the last time, he looked up at the marvellous avalanche, a simple sample of the overwhelming power of the mini-Everests living here, now so impressively tranquil, so natural, so stationary- what a relief. He seemed to slip into more of the attendant shadows…to swim into a womb…why not drop off at a moment's notice?…the snappy yelling pictures would only come back…

Yes, my reverie rests, I'm awake, mate Dr Ash, live on my mobile in the dense human jungle! See! See! Five thousand block bookings, scarcely upright, dotted all over the slopes! Chatterers, shaggerers, wankers, poseurs, selfies, all come in for après ski amid the displays of baseball hats and bats, tiny torn pool tables, drooping college pennants, a jaded juke box full of Bee Gees, old Stones, early Beetles, hits of yester year, 200 selections; tables with stiff steel tubular chairs, fluffy coffee, sucre Arberg, Nidwalden1291,teeny coats of arms, an inverted key with a clover-leaf rampant - wrapped sugar in three languages; by the door a huge imitation Minoan Black Pot with the elaborate ivory handles of elegant umbrellas sticking out. Where was he? What next? Like sheets in the wind, the images puffed and proliferated.

Two lovely girls in skiing gear entered the café with

their Frankenstein boots clumping ominously on the wooden floor. They were beautiful, lithe, chattering away, the only sound. Hang on! Gone. Yes, just a fading police siren, gone now. Back again. The girls do not take the slightest notice as I sit down at a neighbouring table.

"I've been pushed around for long enough" I hear the blond one say, "I want money and power so I can push *them* around for a change." Both nod vigorously. They wear scarves round their necks, gloves on the table, made up to a 'T', their jeans an amazing place, pulled so tight you could make out the cleft and the irrepressible labia – OK with me, but what will their Ma say!

"I'll join a commune and sell roast chestnuts! That'll teach them," says Blondie. "They won't touch us now," her mate says with solemn assurance, tossing her head. Then I notice Blondie's scarf has come loose. I see her neck, front and back, ear to ear, is marked with fresh livid rope burns. I stare in horror as her friend casually throws back her own scarf, she has almost identical livid burn scars - they exchange a look of something akin to conspiracy, as if they had just been cut down. Both adjust the scarves at the same time and with the same movements. Their ghastly wounds are decently covered again.

"I am not going to ring Dad or Mum," says Blondie. "Nor me!" says her sidekick, "checking on us every five minutes, as if we can't look after ourselves!" They exchange four vigorous fives.

"Hey!" Blondie shouts over to me, "come and join us, mate! Nothing's going to happen in this fucking hole today."

I hear more when I don't want to hear more, feel when I don't want to feel, and wish it would stop - like peeing your pants in the dormitory in front of your friends. I had no part in it! Divorce oddity floats up. Yes, that was it. She goes to Istanbul with her husband. Her sister comes with her. All three get drunk and fall into bed. Hubby wakes up in the night sandwiched by cunt to the left, cunt to the right. He reaches out, hangover-randy, finds the familiar naked bum and thrusts inside the back way, not too hard to awaken the sister. He finishes with a sigh and slips off to sleep. Wrong sister, wrong wife, buster! A divorce, both insisted, went on and on and on. The sisters never spoke to each other again. "It was an accident," pleaded the myopic hubby again and again, but they never believed him. Oh, well…"

"Jokes!?" the scene moved over, "there's none here!" delared Nickador.

"So you say!" Karen snapped shut like a Swiss army knife. "Well, I disagree, we do have a sense of humour, even Ma, even Pa, tho he's on the brink of death's door! How we laugh it off, off the cuff, as you say, like when my sister was being fucked in the annex above the garage and grandpa who was on top of her, had to escape - Pa arrived home suddenly – and *his* Pa put on his trousers in a hurry and climbed out of the window onto to the garden-shed roof at the back - and fell into the raspberry canes, his trousers round his ankles and tried to run and fell again, I could see it all from the kitchen window and how I laughed, my sister too, I could hear her laughing all the way to the toilet, then grandpa, every day of sixty-five as you say, hopping like a rabbit till he disappeared into the apple orchard and listen, his trousers still around his ankles. We laughed and laughed like hell, I tell you. Like when you fell off the yacht and smashed your legs against the hull, you should have seen your face, thought you'd broken them. We love jokes, see! Ha, ha, ha, ho, ho, ho! And let me tell you a joke even the English Church Warden told me when I was a child, 'Girl was coming down the London bus from the upper deck and paused on the stairs, "Is it Ealing yet?" she asks the conductor, "No," he replies, looking up her, "needs at least ten stitches!" Ha, ha, ha! Ho, ho, ho!

The laughter tore through the air down into the cellars where it burrowed with the wood lice and the dead daddy-long-legs among the floor-boards, gone, but not for ever or a day, just some time, a little tick… sometime…speaks…fade to the claws of the scuttling sea-floor…! Zzzz…

"Hey, wake up."

"Done! Now, is it true what they say that your **uncle Maurice** is married to an Argentinian harpy called Harriet."

"We just call him, 'uncle' because he's such an old friend.'

"You don't say so."

"Where do you go when people speak to you, my mother thinks you're just a dumb animal sometimes."

"Good old Pa! You don't care if he dies, do you? – not the others up the chimney – just your Pa."

"Not funny."

"After all that happened all that time not so long ago?"

"Nothing to do with you."

"Morals again, is it?"

"Who is this 'Dr Ash who keeps ringing you up on my mobile?"

"He's the man who plays bass guitar in The Shame Of It All, an elusive local rock group in Splott, dead centre of Cardiff, head-quarters of the most magnificent voice in the globe. He's the leader really, eminence blue, insightful as hell, but basically enigmatic, incapable of definition, he possesses tremendous authority, why, nobody quite knows. He's a kind of nagging reminder of better times and of characters of real worth or of all events leading up to the Land of No Shadows. Like me, he has a passion for echoes and reflections, a true son of the People of Daana. There!"

"He's rubbish then, like the rest of your nutty 'friends.' What's his job?"

"He has a degree in Anthropology, or is it Biology?"

"Almost my subject, pharmacology."

"Different application. Anyway, you dropped out of the Uni Course."

"Who cares about this futile echo called Doc Fuckin' Ash? Is he helping you find a job at home."

"No."

"Why all this information he keeps pouring in over here."

"Just the fruits of curiosity."

"Why don't you change your name, everyone agrees

it's ludicrous."

"Sure."

"What?"

"Call me Nick then. You should have mentioned it sooner. Now it' time to drive to **the Clinic**, Pa's Wing. Your Ma's car again, a wreck which she begrudges like everything else she possesses, she's been so kindly towards all her poisonous offspring lately, awful. Have you got the flowers, the unguents, nature's creams, the foot powder…?"

"…I left them for you to get."

"What?"

"Go out and help, go get them! Go! Like Pa always says…"

"Only joking…"

"… Ha, ha, ha! Ho, ho, ho!"

But, as in an aside, Nickador saw there was no twinkle in her eye, and made out just the tip of an adder's tongue between her teeth.

Don't worry, I put it all in the bag in the boot."

"So, ha, ha, ha! Another joke!"

"I saw Julie bearing gifts yesterday, as loaded as a Xmas tree."

"She won't get round Pa!"

"Your nasty Ma thinks you're both tarts."

"For God's sake, not so loud! Anyway, he's fine."

"Your dear old Pa?"

"No, dear healthy young Doctor Klein."

"I shall sleep in Ma's car while I await the inevitable."

"But you're driving."

"Exactly. Then back to our spacious two-roomed hole in the wall, our dear septic-tank called home."

"Shit! Where are we going to live?"

"In some annex or other, who cares?

"Why did you put lilacs in my room?"

"Because the lilacs are in bloom."

"What are you going to do?"

"Snorrr, snorrrrr…something like that…"

"…ha, ha, ha!"

" No one will notice … you'll see…"

"…notice what?"

"The dead of course…"

"What dead…?"

" …of Manorbier, Muridor, Splott, Ash, of course, those lost in avalanches…on the ends of rope…"

"…I'm going out!"

"If you find the Will, do let me know."

"That's not fucking funny! But let me tell you something that is! Pa pulled up once in the drive out there with a crunch, put on the brake, reached over and placed his hand right over my crotch and began rubbing with his middle finger. I loved it, someone else doing it. The first time. I got excited. He slipped off my panties, leaned over and began sucking and licking my labias, til I got the climax. I loved it. **I was only eleven** but I knew what was going on. He used to do that every so often.

What do you think of that?"

"Out you go then! Out! OK? Out!" She left with a puzzled look over her shoulder. Bang went the door.

Nickador's heart subsided. He drooped over his wife's untouchable case. Again, he called for Doctor Morpheus... but buzz, buzz, the mobile, who now? Hi, Ash, just thinking about you. What!? Yes, I got your fucking long lists of queries which I am in the process of answering in detail, and the hard samples, OK? Pirie dishes, yes. Yes, at once, after a quick nod or two. At the Clinic. I have free range, like an egg! Have I ever let you down? – Do not answer that! Thanks for the fresh air, she's out on the town, I don't feel inspired but it closed a few final curtains....off to the last smoke-stack Hostel in the street of Dolours! 'Pick up, Ma, drop off Ma, watch old suck-off Pa going down for the last unforgiving dip. Tell why, why, why? Cheers Ash!' Farewell nobody else!"

Supper with her natural Pa once, months ago, restaurant up in the hills, huge fire for roasting cheese and bar-b-q other choice meats. Her Pa did this. We were just at the dessert stage when he gets up and rushes out to his car. "I'm not going to pay for that rhubarb tart and that old cream! A rip off. Come on! I know where we can get a big and reasonably priced sweet." We all jump in and off we go. We stop at his ex-wife's empty chalet on the lakeside, still in dispute. He parks under a flourishing cherry tree, immense, laden with fruit. He points upwards. The girls clamber up like squirrels and begin picking bunches off the copper-coloured boughs. I look on, cheerful, speechless. Pa ignores me, plucks down a handful of black, over- ripe cherries, chews, pauses, chokes, spits out the skin and pips, weeping through his words.

"Just look at my life! I've failed. Hell! Can't stop that now. I'm fifty-five. I don't have the courage to give up and just leave. I tried that. Came back. Tried to run away with my red-haired mistress. No good. She left me. Failed again." He threw down the innocent fruit, now mingling with his tears, and furiously stamped on them under this wonderful spreading cherry tree. I never saw him again until after his suicide.

Thank God that was quick for me, and for the **poor Cherryman** too, I beg you, Lord of the Flies, Master Lucifer, do not have a sliver of mercy on us! Above all, be quick! Ta, Lord, look, here comes, looming out of the ineffable pastures of the vanished picture palaces of recollection, one Chitti Magayathon of Bangkok, Prince of Smiles, Wizard of the English Language, Mahout, Controller of Elephants and my best ever student. Quite vivid. That's it, speak on, I can make out the mouth, Chitti, say, on autocracy and democracy – yes…no zeezee sleepies while you're here…

CHITTI: "If the people are not clever enough or too

weak to control their employers, they must have someone to take care of them before they become dangerous because of the freedom they have within themselves, otherwise they become like dangerous children, dirty, foul, undisciplined but also kind and loving, silly and ignorant but always a threat because they can bear arms. There are errors everywhere, but it is not liberty to bury the mistakes one makes. No animal has more liberty than the cat but it makes sure it buries the mess it makes. The cat is the best anarchist, humans, the worst. We have much to learn from the cat!"

Chitti, you are as young and clever and gifted as any feline in a pussy box on a marble floor! Your eloquent presence sleeps so well, leaving imprints of extraordinary calm and illumination….zzzz… Cheerszzzz!

A near miss came upon me, that time, as in a leafy suburb with good neighbours looking out for you and some favour fell out of Lady Luck's hands, thanks, somehow… Nickador perceived through a failing mist the For Sale notice was still up outside the front garden gate of the terraced row. Lots of images of the first home of Karen and Nickador. No regrets in the tall grass. He had called to make a final inspection of the rooms. The last sticks of furniture had been removed and he had arranged to switch off the utilities. The gas and electricity Inspectors had reported all in order. Nickador wondered through the upstairs rooms and downstairs, nothing had been overlooked. He went into the kitchen. He examined the plugs and the wiring. He noted the end of the main cooker cable stuck out from the wall, the end taped off. All Ok, as stated. But the cable ought be nipped off, tidier and safer. He took the pliers out of his shoulder bag. At that very instant, he glanced through the kitchen door window, and spotted his popular next door neighbour, Mr Hughes, walking down his garden path to his kitchen. Funny, thought Nick, he always comes in through the front door, a most meticulous gentleman. He waved to Nick and Nick beckoned him to come over. Mr Hughes was never late and never ill. He was an old soldier and had served in the Falklands War and the Iraq campaigns. He had been wounded by a grenade, and still had a limp but still had never been late on parade - a military metronome but an eminently lucky one, a kind of regimental mascot who everyone wanted to be next to, such was his survival value. He now worked on the buses and won the best attendance prize every year. An exceptional man. "Hello there, Mr Hughes!" - he was always addressed as 'Mr Hughes' even by his wife, "come on in." Mr Hughes always called him 'Nick.' "Good to see you. My final visit and check up." Mr Hughes was silent, eyeing the pliers in Nick's hand, he glanced at the protruding cable.

"You're back from work early, I see, Mr Hughes, lucky I caught you."

"Old shrapnel in the bum," said Mr Hughes,

"Foreman sent me home with a doctor's certificate," he held it up like an oily rag, "I wouldn't have come home otherwise. First time for twenty odd years. But my attendance record is still mine." He looked around. "Kept an eye on the place for you, as you asked. Everything OK?"

"According to the last Inspectors."

"Didn't see them," said Mr Hughes, dubiously, "can I help?"

"About to cut the main cable here, just tidying up."

"I saw a couple of viewers round here last night, Nick, and the lights were on."

"Not possible," said Nickador. Mr Hughes reached over and flicked on the light switch. At once the ceiling bulb illuminated every corner of the kitchen.

"Christ!" Nick burst out, involuntarily.

Mr Hughes gently removed the pincers from Nick's hand. "Bless you, Mr Hughes," gasped Nickador, sure he was turning pale, "if I'd cut that cable," he said with a shiver, "I'd now be up flat against that wall, frying like a prime steak…"

…talk the talk, struggling out of creased sheets and

spermy floods, grunts as loud as rutting boars, sighs as....

"...well, when are you going to begin talking?"

"I don't know, it's a big subject."

"Talk the talk now!"

"In a minute."

"Your usual nonsense I suppose, you and your secret, sickening optimisms. You're half drunk again."

"Let's talk sense, the imp of prolixity is in my brain – ' black cabbages, red Brussel sprouts, striped beetroot, brilliant veggies are all different - but brothers in the basket!' - that sort of banter. But let me remind you, no one gets past St Peter at the pearly Gates without a wrinkled forehead! "And how hast thou spent thy time!" he'll ask, the swine. My uncle died quartering sugar cubes, singing 'Onward Christian Soldiers!' swallowed a whole bowl of plums-stones the while, believing they would give him an awfully high."

"This talk has gone on for forty minutes now, haven't you got anything to say to me?"

"This imp of mine has no head but is very talkative – and I *am* using my knife and fork properly. But, no, I admit it, I don't know how to package a gift in the correct manner. That was never meant to be, perhaps."

"You won't last to the end of the week by the sound of it. Why do you always poke your head in the light so I can't see? A **Bucket and Clearance** man, that's all you'll ever be. What? Shut your gob! A "middle–fingered widow" am I? I told you, knock off the crap. What? 'you and your stupid old black angel with scarlet wings'? - that crap again? So 'apples never fall far from the tree,' so go and shit in the hole in the sofa then and wipe your arse on the Daily Telegraph, that's all the funnies you're good for. Humour? We laugh like mad in this circle of old friends and relations, I can promise you. Didn't my best friend go for a holiday and come back to find her hubby had built a wall in the sitting room in their apartment, no door, cutting the space in half, they didn't want to sell it, she lived one side of the wall and he on the other and all just because he said they had become strangers-in-the night - to each other. They paced up and down separately for the rest of their days. That is a real funny. Hear me laughing now, I can hardly stop, I tell you, that story kept the entire family in laughs for months. 'Humour?' Ha… ha…ha…ho…ho…ho…"

He exits the scene effortlessly with the aid of Remy Martin - an ex-pat Taff, an anonymous passing silhouette at Tesco's liquor counter opposite the Grandville apartment, changes his mind, buys instead a packet of sweet digestive biscuits, goes down to the edge of the lake and begins **feeding the ducks** in the moonlight. A police car pulls up, Big Cop comes out, and arms akimbo, demands, "And what do you think you're up to, son?" 'Son' crumbled another biscuit and throws it into the water. He stands up to his full height, five foot seven, and says in his best high bourgeois accent, "I am feeding the ducks, Officer. See." He throws bits of biscuit into the calm waters. "Like that. Quack,quack! The ducks are flying low to night. Good night, Officer."

"Yes...good night...sir." Another blasted nut. No point making a report. Might be well connected, it's that accent, you never knew these days with these fucking rich illegal fugitives. Where do they all come from? Yes, 'quack, quack!' boded no pleasure for him.

Tonight the skeletons of yester-year are ringing the bells of remembrance for tomorrow's harvest of dead. Baudelaire's last words were, "the moon is pretty." And he was right, never even slightly off-key.

Somewhere he slumped down into the phantasmagoria of his jumble-jostled brain, The acid eye-wash of the family drained away down the plug-hole of a tabula rasa, anyway. Yes, mumbo, jumbo – farewell! To think...I was called 'angel' once... yes, 'angel' I said. I trail off, so...where are you...zee... zees...?

Snap the fingers, raise the elbow - **the Guinness that**

exploded immediately comes to mind. A bit smudgey! Key lost at midnight. Pull sleeve down over hand, aim for the glass panel next to the lock, and – bash! The pane splinters and he is inside. His pal falls in behind him. They were in his small rented flat in arrears by the hundreds. Pat, Irish hoer of beet and loquacious poet, staggered in carrying the crate of Guinness. Nick began his Winter coughing again, hard dry barks mixed with hoarse grunts, cutting pains in the lungs, as if he'd swallowed a scimitar. "Have ye fixed in a second ," says Pat, as Nick subsided. "Me old Mam's recipe, cured stallions and bulls by the dozen she did, well known in County Kerry. Where's the stove? Got to be on the boil. Saucepan?" Nick handed him his worn out Woolworth's receptacle and poured a few foaming bottles into it. He stopped after the fourth and tested the libation with a lick of the finger. He nodded. He turned up the gas. Pat regulated the flame with a keen eye. Just at that point Nick began yet another heaving bout of hacking and rasping, spluttering and spitting, didn't know what. They turned away from the stove as Pat slapped Nick fearlessly on the back. He gave one gigantic heave - and at that very moment, the Guinness exploded! In an instant, both were dripping with the famous black Irish stuff! Nick could hardly make out his old friend and the stove was swimming in running *liquide noire*. The ceiling too was also hit spot on, a huge dripping ring of the best Dublin brew showered down on us. The saucepan clattered back to earth, black as a coffin. Pat suddenly threw a wondering glance at his friend, Nick threw one back, lips at the ready. Gulp, gulp! Yes, they realised in the same instant that Pat's Mam and her herbalistic hedge spells had done their magic - no damn cough, anywhere, in body or mind! Just an empty vacuum of a chest without a tickle in it! No doubt of it. Nick at once felt terrifically well and very stalwart. 'Good for you, Mam Ireland ,' he cried out, 'from over there in distant County Kerry, you have cured a benighted Silurian soul over this side of the oceanic tribal divide!' The two friends realized, as one, that whether the Guinness was in the pan or flying free, didn't matter! She, the Mother of Moyvan and Matron of horrendous Coughs, had made him whole again. He felt a long-lasting gratitude rise up in his soul and his throat, 'bless you, emerald Mam of Pat, Earth Goddess of Holy Guinness !' he prayed, fervently reaching for the next libation. There was still plenty of Guinness left to celebrate the occasion!

Whispers as well as pictures flicker on and off in the gloaming, showers of life-giving sunlight over the impossibly green bournes, along with longtime vanishments of bruised untreated memories…bollocks again…whisssshhhhper – like that…Zzzz…

The **epidemic of suicides** progesseth wondrously, almost of its own perdition. "Why, lovely to see the bar-b-q fires at both ends of the town bridge with volunteer celebrants at the ready. Part of the festive season, eh!?"

"No, idiot, it's to stop the jumpers. So often the bodies crash through the roof of the forecourt of the garage below, Insurance company refuses to insure anymore, so it's closed now, just the blood stains left. You wouldn't think," she said with a laugh, ha, ha! "that the insurance companies are actually saving up human lives, collecting bodies, a bloody travesty if you ask me. No ha, ha for that! And we used to hear the screams from the school as they went down. Didn't do anything about *that*, did they?"

… it all echoes like bats' wings' slithering down the rooves of fathomless, murky caverns. Out of the-sometime-or-other fumes of the distorted cocktails of recollection, , poor, quavering, desperate **'uncle-in-law' Maurice**, rises into view as from under every black cloud going. Poor flattened Maurice, come on up, five foot six, skinny as a pea-pole; sunken cheeks; eye holes, shrivelled slits; occasional glints, absolutely nowhere, except despair; rare eater, ever drinker, rough red Algerian stuff, inert as a possum; razor-faced wife Harriet from the Pampas of cougar and pole-cat - boss of her table. Three sons, on right, left hand. Maurice, far end, alone, hardly living or dead. In daily time, a Council bin man, never his own team man, never his own trash. She, the Countess of Harriet, ruined beautician of the Argentine, now all wifey daggers-drawn, forever; bitterness set in stone, permanently sharpening her fangs on useless fucking Maurice; three sons, when and where unknown, all gay. Tim, dancer of ballet; Mike, student of medicine, local uni; Gerry, deaf-mute; Tim, bearer of bad news. Dinner talk for four, never one for thin mad Maurice. Maurice in attic, banished, centuries ago. Harpy-Ma nods. The eldest Tim grunts, writes message on pad, passes it on. Brothers add more messages. Pass back to Pa, Pa reads, burst into tears, rushes upstairs. Laughter from family four. Ha, ha, ha! Ho, ho, ho! The message, 'Failure,' it reads, every time. 'Failure! Failure! Failure"! Ma nods, her voice like barbed wire strands pulled through tin-cans. She'd tell him, the family, the world. How him! Tim collected the messages every Friday. Tim son not so dumb. Creakings from attic room. Pauses looking upwards. Throws open Pa's old attic door. Beholds skinny Pa-Maurice hanging from tow-rope of Harriet's-volkswagon, looped over beam. Maurice stood but once on that chair, put on noose, kicks away. All just once. Body in rigour found, a week late, no messages for Maurice, received or sent this time. Last testament as one from the house of the bewildered – Corporation Department to have all estate, with proviso that his, mad Maurice's, body, be left to the Uni Medical Faculty for dissection by students of that year, including Mike, with Gerry, Tim, Mother as dearly beloved witnesses. No cash bequests. Harriet explodes with mirth, of course not, she'd transferred all his council wages over to her own account years ago. She'd had a word with the medical director too, and after the big flare up, the final blood-boil, the cut-price cremation would do OK, no useless autopsy for Mr Flat Anonymous, no one there, hole in the air, the last of the trash of Maurice to a 'T' – but Maurice got an **urn burial** after all, right in Tim's empty fag-tobacco box, in went the ashes! which tin later joined the stained coffee percolaters of life in the Corporation rubbish tip. Harriet, in one single tremendous ejaculation of spite, as furious as pyroplastic flow from a volcano – bade her last farewell – and ordered a simple tulip, slightly drooping, to be kept in a silent jar, not to be scattered at the last hello, except by herself!

Zzz…buzz…zzzeee… What on earth..?! The image of poor solitary, tulip-dangling Maurice swept onwards to the final droop…one petal to go…to the ultimate shade of pale… lots more inhabited bubbles high on nostalgia, whoever, wherever, thank you Dr Ash!… *Zzzzz Zzzz* to **the Bank and the Wren** dropped in. Nickador looked out of trolley-bus number 56 at the myriad waiting zombie-suits; sunshine drooped like a dead weight onto the necks of the season-ticket victims – yes, we were in a banking metropolis alright, the land of the drooping mouth, the clenched anus, the unreturned feeling – literal-minded to the point of imbecility. A teaching colleague had told him the night before how delighted he was with his bare new gums because they saved so much money, not having to buy false teeth actually, that is. Woe to those with only material incentives! Nickador felt vaguely disturbed. Yes, as he gazed out of his brown study, he remembered, he had to go to the bank, the one identified by a row of Himalyan Silver Birches in front of its immense portals - which trees outside echoed with a single ecstatic bird of extraordinarily sweet song– it only takes one! Perhaps the birches and their brotherly feathered friend would ease him out of his worm-wood and gall mood. Earlier that morning, Nickador had felt the radio story of the beheading of an unlettered apprentice somewhat unsettling. Perhaps that was it. At college, the day before, he had been bold enough to tell another of his fellow lecturers, Dr Papanda, that mankind just could not keep wandering all over the globe wiping their arses on the Book of Revelations, without expecting a comeback! Dr Papanda had added that it was a national disgrace for young people to hear such outrageous comments coming from the staff room. "I now only write psychological assessments for disturbed adolescents," he reminded Nickador testily, although he had, he confessed, "devoted his entire life in the struggle for free cremations for all. "Nickador descended the purring punctuality machine, the bus, walked past the line of Himalayan birches, the first of which housed that favourite song-bird of his, a tuneful mini Jenny Wren it was after all! - who was also, as he had already told another colleagues, a compulsive cheerful sitter in the white trees, not just a sad little flier between them. Nickador whistled to his melodious pal as he passed underneath the vast front entrance and the bird whistled back, no doubt wishing him good luck for the nonce. Nickador at once perked up. Jenny Wren was doing it, conveying the message of good will today to a greying old sympathiser! He grinned as he passed the monumental marble columns. The bank was as big as a space-rocket hangar. The bank manager had told him already that a joint account would enable his wife to walk away with his earnings in her handbag if she felt like it, as women were wont to do, apparently. Nickador had mildly reminded the Manager that he had married his wife because he trusted her, however eccentrically, not the opposite. The bank manager had given up at that point - these innumerate odd-ball know-it-alls from abroad! Immigrants by the dozen, and all unfit for purpose, banking purpose especially! At the next counter a more normal scene seemed to be ensuing. A client had requested paper money in exchange for a pile of saved gold coin he had extracted from a money belt under his shirt. He had received, in exchange, half a stack of crisp 10000 Swiss franc banknotes. The client clutched the pelf, becoming electrified on the spot! He leapt onto the counter, hanging onto the bars of the grille, waving the divine crinkly lettuce for public inspection, "Look! Look! Aren't they beautiful!" He crunched up the notes. "Hear that?! Music, pure music? Hear it? Well, it's mine, all mine!" He pointed to the portrait on the notes, "look! Perfect, our own William Tell! All so beautiful. All saved for a rainy day! I am that rainy day! All for me! Beautiful! Today! Monday!" He was still shouting "beautiful!" when the heavily armed security guards escorted him out. What a bore, observed the Bank Manager, the show-off millionaire addle-brain always did that on the first day of the week, as if he had just been born. Twat!" he added, as his glance fell on

Nickador. Yes, he mused, all non-bourgeous clients were lunatics, mad distraught outlander rejects. He himself was the sole survivor of many a coin skirmish, which fact emphasised his perspicuity as well as his courage. After all, was he not the Director of the whole gleaming emporium from the inside as well as the outside, to the end of his thousand -year contract? - the longest in the commune's history, he had no hesitation, just look around! Boss all over it!

Nickador stood under one of the white birches and waved good bye to his fluttering, chirpy mate, feeling restored, revived by the song, which had hit the spot! He caught the next **number fifty-nine** to his institutional place of utterly pointless pedagogical duties. Nothing untoward happened along the way –a refreshing change…Zzz…zzz...

SNOWY PEAKS! Karen whooshed to a halt, a flurry of snow in her wake, irritated by Nickador's sudden stoppage in front of her. Karen had been skiing since childhood and often left him behind as she disappeared at high speed under the snowy boughs of the pine trees crowding the slopes. Nicador had insisted on their coming, even out of season and they had been lucky – a huge fall of late season snow. She paused. What was the irritating novice of a husband up to now? Nick remained fixed to the spot, gazing far out, spell-bound as the full orb of the morning sun burst between the peaks of the far mountains across the endless plunging valleys. The flood of light spread over the snowy savannahs in great waves, now bright, now dark, shadows chased by the winds between the shining peaks. A huge snow burst spilled over the closest summit, far above the mortal pistes and mutable skiers. The mass tumbled over the slopes, smothering the rocky landscape in a vast coverlet of thick, shifting cotton wool. The mini-avalanche of snow and cloud slowed and ground to a halt. Were all avalanches as beautiful? Nick gasped at the sheer, huge, spectacular, endless brilliance of it. He exhaled ecstatically. Heavens, he thought, I am breathing in the breath of the immemorial, pristine, snows! I am drinking in the very milk of paradise!

"Why," he heard her voice behind him, "why do people ever want to get married?"

In a flash, he switched to another out-of-order sign, – why do people always want to get buried? Was it? Who knows? Sleep on it. Ha, Ha!…Zzzz… **Funerals**: … another merciless shaking out! The Lady of the Bedraggled Tulip shook the blossom in time to her sobs. – "ah!" "oh!" Shake, shake. She stared at the coffin under her feet. "Ah" "Oh!" and raised the ghost of a bruised blossom, a little yellow tulip, just one petal still hanging on, she waves as if to throw it in. Hell, yes, I saw it, second sight, I changed it, how one image gives birth to another, instantly, there, and no charge. There again! All my own dear metemorphoses! from a one-petal to a whole galaxy of gardens, cascading down the fancy-free highway of the horticultural dream - spreading wide as a waterfall, note the tumbling classy celandines, the shiny, dog-mercury foliage for background, the very imaginative, even stunted little groundsels, with their drooping heads, flakes of ergot in the mini-sheaves of wheat, now the Lilies of the Valley with their fleshy orange-red berries, I behold, I done it on purpose, all laid out in concentric circles, very artistic, O, the Pythagorean measures there! - with Monkshood, not forgetting old Oleandor, the breast Killer, and Rhododendron side by side with panther Mushrooms for skin absorption, no bleeding error, healthy in their own habitat; on you fall, death caps and all, so obvious, give the game away, all did their odorous floral duties with finality! Oh, beware the Paternoster pea now arriving on platform six, the precatory bean, black-eyed Susan from her wild licorice Pontefract roots, locks dyed in blue-berry blue, what a falling off was there! - the mass tumbled over the vertiginous edge into the water-misty clouds. 'I had a dream...' And the Lady of the Tulip back to earth, in wrath and rage, hurls the dead tulip down, and see! - it hits the coffin plate and bounces off! - to earth, sweet root! The Lady ceases her moanings and salty tears, in frustration, she has not seen it all as it was meant to be seen, as Ma and her maggoty brood saw it, – every flower, branch and brow, bough and bark, all highly deleterious to any of the human species, like her ex-husband in the hole, and she had not seen it work, just the falling bloody rope trick. All, every vestige, was ruined loveliness. No doubt of it. Later, she whirled around in the café Mirador so her skirts flared outwards and upwards just to show her new boy-friend her cunt was still open for business. Bless you, lady, you were the star of the show, ugly beyond redemption as you are, not that stinky sweaty prick of a man of yours enfolded in his terminal suit of unmeasured clay! Failures all are men, yes, true! No**! the Cherryman** you mean? How's that for answers. Dr Ash I have to report, trail is getting hotter, do I pass the test? No matter. Again, she whirls till she is a spinning shadow, a quiver of quims, outta sight, like, man …Zzzz! for God's sake, Dr Ash, knock it off for once, willya! I am not troubling you, so……Zzzz…Zzzz…to… Gunman at Table!

The Lebanese waiter sailed over to my accustomed table where I was taking a break with two or three of my stand-offish colleagues . The Waiter was slender, slight even for all that, with short weasel-sharp features, a wary but ready smile. He waved his hands a lot.

"As I was saying yesterday - at home in Beirut," he plunged on without pause, " I used to practice on the Parking signs opposite the family home," he mimed shooting a pistol, " – one bullet just after the 'P' then another after 'a' to the end. I got good at it, they had plenty of signs, and my Ma was pleased, said it made her feel safe – until the bastards, they're not terrorists, just thieves and robbers, burned down our little home, a Christian home, blood-thirsty Muslims! Anyway, my church sent their priests too, they had plenty of guns.

Everyone knew that I'd killed the Allah Akbar assassins, didn't last two minutes, I was a sharp-shooter by that time. Came home one night, in the opposite direction I usually took, and as I approached I saw the guy crouching by the boot of my car. Well, I was ready. I raised my gun, he, his. He steadied and fired. I felt the bullet whine under my ear. I aimed for his thigh, the femoral artery, "Put the gun down!" I yelled. He raised it. Just as rapidly, I aimed for a disabling shot in the thigh and fired – and hit him in the eye. Before the police arrived, I'd searched the dead swine, and located my gold bars in the money-belt underneath his sweater. He had been so confident, the shit. Going to wave them under my nose, was he? Goading me on? Little did he know I was by that time the champion sniper of the whole Christian community - with a reputation for fair play. Respect! With my two gold bars, I bought my dearest mother a little house in a quiet suburb of Beirut. She says she now feels safe and comfortable again and wants to die there, her new home.'

Now, gentlemen, how can I help you?"

I fall into the next frame…**a crappalogue on Poverty** believe it or not - and snap into an awake state, God, it slaps you in the face, a huge thump and the all-threatening terror of poverty fills your body, soul and ballocks. Someone screams, "I am so poor, so piss poor!" But no way out of the black tunnel of empty pockets. You wriggle down to the bottom sheet and curl up in foetal position, hiding your head so the kapo-bailiffs won't notice their nark is in an advanced state of decomposition. Nickadore wails silently. 'How long am I going to be so piss-poor? How long to tremble when there's a knock on the door; the stomach knots, on and off, the nausea of the penniless again culminates in a grinding guts' ache! - How long will I be in this painful straining shitting mode?' Lady Luck tells all the universe warningly – 'you wait, ha, ha! Poverty has her little surprises and cruel devices;' the sun also rises but he's still in the thrall of bank statements and solicitor's letters are the only reality; he burrows deeper like a frightened rat into a pile of fat, no way out, just drowning in bile, all the livelong while, makes him incontinent, makes him void - his whole being milked by the Hag of Poverty shrieking at the twerp at the bottom of the bed – the poor sleepmate of the Agony of Skint!" Was that her Ma or Pa on his wretched mobile now ? "Wherever you hide, don't you worry, some train will come along from far and wide and smash you into bits the day you died! Ha, ha! Or you could just become a jumper, a Cherryman of the day, any day!"

"Bollocks! But thank you for dropping in so unexpectedly."

Dr Ash's voice broke in insistently.

"Ok, Nick, but just ease back on the angst stuff, Nick! OK?"

"But my apt phrases and accurate observation are as golden oranges in frames of silver, are they not?"

Whangh! - a half empty screen, now a full one…

"…junk!" said Karen, 'settling a pillow by her head.'"

"I was thinking…"

"…for God's sake, change the subject!"

"I keep seeing Gardens of Paradise with real toads in."

"Why ask me?" Nick staggers out of bed in the two bare lying charity rooms and prances around Kate's unbending body.

"'I am your man, and you are my lady…' Let's dance. I've just come from the Black Kat."

"You've run to the bottle again, haven't you?! You are pissed as usual."

"There was this guy, not ours before who was such a laugh, give or take nine or ten o'clock, and he suddenly **jumps onto the table**, unplugs the bulb, sticks in his own machine, turns up high and yells ! "Listen to the music, love the music, be the music, dance to the music, be the Mariachi of life like your own babeee…" The waiters dragged him down and threw him out, his fucking illegal tablet after him, still mariaching through the air-waves. And like on many occasions, and remember I'm just only a tiny bit pissed, I seemed to be the only one singing and dancing and loving to the three guitars of life, the sombreros, the duende, and the sol-y-smbre of it all, like it was my own babeee…"

"Look at you! Balls! What a joke! What a failure!"

"I am still laughing, tho' my heart is jumping ..."

"…get an etiquette book, learn manners, I've told you! This craziness will get you nowhere."

"Got it! Chiquito! Fernando! Actualization is when you *are* the moment of fleeting inspiration, call it what you will!"

"Why in the hell *do* people want to get married?! I asked before!"

"A desperate effort to avoid dying alone, I suppose."

"And you never told me?!"

"No laughing matter, my darling! Ha, ha!"

"You **are** drunk. "

"Not only do I have nostalgias by the dozens, I have a good half hundred zanies to fall back on, so there, that's true!"

"Brainless drunken crap. Get into bed, or get out of my life!"

"You on the juice too? Never mind. After the flying Mariachi conductor had quit the premises, I seized one of those big Swiss cheese finger things, gripped it like a Smith and Wesson, and went round, table to silent table, crouching like Sergio Leone at the OK corral, and warning them, "handy hoch or I'll fill you full of cheese!' This guaranteed my sejour in the fleeting chambers of Parnassus riding on thin air! Out I went too!" Sorry, a bit too long there. Ha, ha, ha! Ho, Ho, Ho!"

"Shut the fuck up!"

"Appalling fucking cliché there! One last word first: 'Old men, wise men, good men, wild men, grave men, all you singing, dancing nuts out there, bless you with these fierce tears I pray…!...""

Jesus, what is it? Why was I ever born with such a head? I move just one step from my floor and where do I come out? In dwindling floods of unnamed portraits from the land of fading nowheres! My worlds, my agonies, my poverties, my mistakes! Let me please escape, I've had enough of this fucking jape. Bless Manobier! Minervia! Go, go, go! Help, someone, help, help!"

"No!"

It goes all fuzzy, no hard edges again, I grab my mobile and make for the hidey-hole.

Back safely in the **den of Concierges**, I remarked that from this morning the dreadful Ma had changed practically overnight. The old Hag told cow Karen we could use the storage room in her home if we were ever short of space. What about Pa's the two rooms he puts it about he's letting us have for free till we're fixed up, a lie to bolster his reputation as a real Christian, no doubt. But if that lie came out, wouldn't that damage poor rotting Pa? Hag just told me to drive her and Julie and Karen to the Clinic as if I was a member of the family, 'please use my car when you will!' We all clambered in, smothered in highly-coloured blossoms as usual, hardly the suitable thing for a man who can hardly register one shade of gray. On arrival, Doctor Klein insisted on peace and quiet, sshh, sshh…finger on lip, the fake snake, hold back in the toilet area, he ordered, tranquillity even, no church bells, no more Christ's mother in the slums of Jerusalem, no more sullen suffocating bar-b-q's in gardens. No more Smoking areas. And the dutiful ladies agreed, not even a poke in the eye with a dry stick, and that included not only tight-lipped Julie but my worse half as well, with her melting sneer. They were so hushed, it was momentous! Had they buckled under to the sweet reason of Dr Bloody Klein? I awaited the inevitable throwback! It zoomed in on sticky wings, right into my current bewilderment, I was also rewarded for my patience and pains with two hours a week more at the local Technical College, an extraordinary slip of the pen by the thumb-screw of a Director. I kip-drive, brain dead as the ladies continue

uncannily…silent…what you suggest Dr Ash? ZZZZZ….ZZZZ…good enough! Yes, stick up in the Rue de Bourg flashes and holds: My fellow pal was one**, Tan, a south Vietnam refugee**, out of the ravaged coconut trees into the limelight…strange…no, not so. Chitti and Tan, sort of ineffable, hard and kind… We both loved the films of Sergio Leone, especially *Once upon a Time*. We knew Clint's 'draw' to the last centimetre, and would often 'draw' on each other in the staff room. This time it was in the Rue de Bourg, town centre. I crouched. Tan crouched. He whirled his gat, I fingered back the hammer of mine. I aimed. He aimed, thumbs all cocked. Suddenly, a hulking body all suit and dark glasses, crashed between us. The figure whirled around like Bruce Lee, stepped back, and pulled open his jacket. There, snuggling in a shoulder holster, was a real neat Beretta 007. "Don't nobody move!" he snarled at me in particular with a pseudo yank accent, "or it's curtains." The hulk then lifted me off my feet and placed me carefully out of Tan's way. "You OK, Tan?" he asked, Tan nodded, "OK this side of paradise, Dominique! Great to see you in action again."

"Is that thing real?" I could not help asking about the weapon." Dominique flipped open the chamber, "fully loaded! See my tie? What does it say? NYPD, me, seconded from the International Police Agency here for years to New York, Tan was my guide and mentor, his advice to move onwards and outwards and upwards, words of perfection, Chief Detective now, Head of Aliens Department. Never forget that, guy, whoever you are - anyone who draws on Tan, draws on me! OK?" He embraced Tan again. "Let's go for a beer, Tan. You coming," he asked me.

What could I say, Dominique had the gun.

Back to business later, some geography spread out and would not leave me alone! I come to out of sleep on a bed surrounded by highly-coloured tents, stalls of mounting fruit, display trays of spreading pomegranates, pyramids of plums, and a single gushing 'non potable' spring in the middle of the Square for all not to drink from. Quite astonishing. It was true! Voices chatter like a thousand rattle-snakes in the foothills of the High Sierras. It is a barely human fucking **Market Day**, what a a difference - one devoted to a huge exhibition of primitive, primordial 'artisanal' work, all carved out of the finest local timber, freshly felled, like so many of the population, displayed to the world. The whole of the

County was represented there right down to the smallest village, which sometimes offered the largest vanity carvings in this wholly weird other-worldly communal fruit-and -nut event. Together, the arty goods on display covered the entire Square with centuries of the most famous of biblical annals depicted in the Holy Scriptures, such as the Creation and the Flood, as two main themes. The first sculptured figure Nickador approached was of a naked man crouching, his head bent down so he could stare backwards through his bowed legs, a permanent expression of diabolic glee on his face; a second nude character sat on the back of his mate gazing down at him with the same intense evil grimace; both figures were covered with thick, matted carved hair, white-back gorillas – not descendants of the shining 'Adam' couple, surely not the aboriginal originals?! Dotted around, in lighter though darker vein, were fluttering, ferocious, fairy figurines in hideous Halloween masks - were these the 'Eves ' in the genesis book? Next, he found himself standing in Noah's procession of shuffling animals, only a couple feet high, at most, all queuing up to enter the Arc, a futuristic ocean liner which looked like a gigantic amphibious fifties Amercan Buick. The line stretched on up and up the artificially-raised slopes, impossibly steep, all called 'Arrarat.' Nickador looked with astonishment at the scarlet- coloured pairs of hippos and giraffes, and hundreds of other species, guarded by pairs of brilliantly caparisoned mercenary mediaeval Byzantine pikemen, as at the Battle of Jericho. Thousands of pairs of irreligious decapitated corpses strewed the Tuscan landscape. The papal Swiss Guard, even then, saved the Vatican City, which always reminds us with its yellow leggings, and, no doubt, of the suns of Van Goch's pineapples - hues exoticissimi, at about fifty million a kick in oils! On a raised platform, fresh out of water, lay pairs of monstrous sea-creatures, teeny weeny floppy squids stretched out as if in a permanent yawn, yuck; conger eels with a bite like a cougar, leading up into the watery clouds with pines, every branch an exclusive visage sprite in wood. What a come back, quel cauchmar! A t the front of one of the myriad stalls, by the very portals of the Empyrean, stood one of the pieces of resistance, a purple and mauve pair of boars, flanked by brown dawn cockerels, their anal feathers splayed out proudly, crowing to the sties. Yes, even ants and ant-eaters were there, in equality, in serried ranks all under the influence of God who had brought them here to worship the Lord and be saved from the coming dip in the infernal round pond in the last circle or so of Hades. Thus was the world laid out in highly sensitive circular articles of faith and unbelievable spiral mathematics, everything in sight arranged with the deadly tedious tidiness of an SS firing squad. Zeig Heil, mates! The stalls stretched onwards remorselessly, a steadfast tribute to the Arc and all who sailed in her. Nickador suddenly recoiled. He was at the very altar of the moulded wooden magnificencies, and he could still be taken aback like that? The Holy Fount stood there like a reformed, denuded Tower of Babel revealed in all the guilty aftermath of a wet dream! What more proof of the Deity was there needed, at any time, at any age?!? But Nickador perforce, sniffed again, deeply, the fool was full of hope, again, nothing like an old one, and coughed until he was flat on the floor and quite purple. Some bloody nasty vapour had got to him. He scuttled to the edges of the crowds of pairs of prophets, visionaries and seers, and ancient fakes, St Peter the Parody, Paul the Preposterous, the coming Trinity and the Holy Spook, but he did not want to strain his nostrils with a second niff. Yes, he now knew well enough that all the sensitive 'artisinal' creations had been liberally creosoted so the whole live-long display reeked of spilled industrial diesel. Now the last exhibits, deadwood carvings of ancestors on cracked frames, were being strung up to the simulacrum of a gallows by an unsmiling crew of teenagers, male and female, with pony tails. Surely, Nickador reflected, this ghastly spectacle clearly represents the ugliest and most odious aspect of mankind's First coming, let alone Second, here in this common or garden Saturday citizens' market place, near the glittering lake where the MacDonald's sky-scrapers rise to the heavens and stand forever in elevated acts of vast fiscal creation, like the eucharist, a bit, where humanity is never shamed and deep dollar-joys and gold-brick adorations always pile up in private corporate soul-cellars, so decent, so respectable, so universally beloved, so emulated by the gods themselves! Oh, Ash yourself - whence in hell did this irrapturous fever spring?!

"For Christ's sake, save me, Chitti, I'm falling to pieces and each piece is going nutty. I say." Nickador now became convinced it was not time to hit the zee zees but to get really, right royally plastered. It was not a long trip with his old Ma's box camera put away in the drawer for a while. But it soon reverberated all the way back! Pix, pix, like that. No good hiding place! The most unwelcome Exhibition of the ghastly market was faded out with a kick and a grunt! No more! Zeeeeeeeeeeeeeee… Twinkle, twinkle little star…ha, ha! No, not another NAGALOGUE!?

"We have to talk," insisted Karen, quite de-composed, "of course I sometimes think of him, after all he is my lover. Why aren't you like him? Never mind. Why do you always sing "it's all over now baby blue" about us? Sex never meant much. Why don't you see that this is serious for me? And those socks do not go with your shoes. Go now? Why do you always plan like a machine, 'chop, chop, chop' like that?' you said, "I do not like Bristol, I got a blister in Bristol." All you could say was, "I do not feel like talking to night." So what? What's in the mail? Another rejection? Another failure!? Like the eternal Cherryman? Well, don't blame me!" she said, "My lover is brilliant. Brilliant!"

"A moon is brilliant, a glacier is brilliant, stars and diamonds are brilliant, but a 'lover'? Never!"

"That is what you said last night!"she said, "spare me

the repeat."

"Beware the great gray Stabiliser!"

"I need a dictionary when I talk to you."

"Let's celebrate your birthday soon, then."

"You can't celebrate everything," she snapped, "you are in a private world when you dance, no one can get through and it is even worse when you're writing."

"Don't worry, I am now searching for a meaningless relationship!"

"Ha, ha, ha!"

"I'm off for a mountain-path walk."

"Good, I suppose. You said last night if you remember, you fool, that if I was Queen of Sheba, it would still be 'poor little me' for me."

"True!"

"Don't talk so quietly," she shouted, "there's no one else in the room! You and your sickening secret optimisms!"

"Look for the shitty lining, all part of the skid marks

of life, I say! but tell me, O Lord, where to go, what to do, I need to inform someone in authority that nothing down here works."

"You are as out of date as just a pair of old red braces," she said, "and do not fall out of that apple tree there, you may damage the branches."

Ta. Time for a whole bottle of Calvados, time for failing fast. All this, every picture, something to do with me? Ask Doc Ash! No, this just came back...

Twinkle, twinkle little star, how I wonder what you are,

Up above the world so high, like a diamond in the sky,

Twinkle, twinkle...

Another bold **bourgeois arse-tight scene** or reception slips into mind - a block of huge sliding glass panels, with roomy open spaces all round, every inch a hideous expense, with real pictures - God is this a Miro, and that a Klee, never a Matisse cut-out! I gasp for a drink. I sit on an enormous puffed up sofa, just like the owners. I behold glass-topped tables with reflecting magazines, polished mohogany floors beneath me, drapes of Aztec design for the draughts. I go out onto the towering terrace with a view of the lake in heavenly mode. The gaily coloured canopy flaps refreshingly in the breeze. A graveyard is not prettier but the inhabitants are livelier. No, shit, you must not intrude! Little old almond and caviar tit-bits appear on crystal trays, carried by sleek Italianate garcons. I take a bite of the salami and slide the rest into my pocket. It tastes like soggy soap, and in such a setting.

"What a wonderful idea to have a party in an art gallery," I say to Karin.

"This isn't an art gallery," she hisses back, "this is their living room."

The moon is up and I am out. Lovely! There are bushes, hedges, ditches, drains to hide in, the very ones I have just come out of. Nasty old clouds sailing down, hiding nothing. Don't feel like filling in the blanks today…except for the **Hydra Romance Menu** memory, clear as a painted bell. She'd bought postcards of the Greek Isle of Hydra, addressed them, written her messages, addressed them and - had forgotten to send them. He picked one up. It was to her hag Ma, now a changeling, of all people. She never generally bothered with messages to Ma. The second she read was for her new boy-friend, no doubt. 'The test is working. I've been with him, I've slept with him and I can't lie, he was so kind to me, kindness I cannot say 'no' to. He even ran a bath or me. I've decided to stay with him although we're still married. I'll always remember what you did for me, helped me to grow up, to face myself.' The front of the card was in the shape of one big heart with the word 'love' written all over it. "Let's meet at our special restaurant, Vincent's, again. Did I tell you, Vincent is known all the way from here to the Moulin Rouge, a two-star Michelin chef, but all my French friends say he deserves at least four stars. Didn't our last week-end confirm it? Such quality, the Coteau Vigne Blanche de Cologny! And the Carte is not fixed either, but that's not important if you want to be avant-garde. And Oh! The Langouste a l'americiane, the turbotine aux petite legumes, the fois de canard aux capres, out of the top drawer, superb! Yes, cherie, Vincent's restaurant exists to celebrate all the great occasions of life, the sad ones too. We could even call this parting a second honeymoon. A kiss for our double lives."

"My love," she murmured as they slipped into bed together.

"A sex and food hagmologue again, a come-back as clear as a mirror on your horizon of nasty nostalgias? Christ, you must be running out of jerk-offs, Nickador!"

"Did you hang up my bra and panties? Where's my red dress? Wash these again, the spoons are still greasy. Don't do it that way, you clean everything wrong. Like living with a small child, I hate your curtains. Why sleep in your clothes? What's that? A toy canoe? Looks like a coffin. So you've done the shopping, only think of your appetites, don't you? Make sure the roofer uses the right cement. I couldn't stand looking at you eating, for five months. And earn something. Buy a book, how to influence people, no more stupid students, like Chitti. I hate the work you do in the garden. Do you want me not to tell the truth? I'm frigid as a birthmark. I've given up sex with other men. No, I haven't. You've got no conversation so we don't talk. You and your artistic emotions. Takes me days to recover from a bad blow-job. What you mean - ? "Mother of God from the slums of Jerusalem?" You said that once, yes, running out. Not funny at it now. I am ashamed of my one-night stands. No, I am not. I feel like a fuck in front of the TV. No I do not. My last one turned me on, then What do you know about my orgasms? Practically nothing. I am so awful, it hurts. It came to me right out of the blue like all my boy-friends, why two weeks ago none of them were even on the skyline, they turned me on, then off, like a guilty thing. I still love you. But why should I deny myself the pleasure. I wish I'd had a thousand lovers, but I don't suppose you'd have liked that. How was my trip? Well I didn't go to bed with anyone, if that's what you mean. I've got a sex block on you. Your hand on my belly, like a tarantula, all hairy legs. I've no experience, right, so how should I get it then? You do not know what makes me tick. It's all out of my hands, I didn't do it on purpose. I need 'external stimuli' the Doc said, especially when I'm with you. I'm like a pin-cushion and I want to know how many pins I can take. Twenty per cent is nothing, but the cushion's filling up nicely.

My Ma and me are getting closer. A mother and daughter thing, you wouldn't understand. Above all, I need affection, every day, and kindness too. Mumble, mumble, what did you say?"

"May many tons of deeply-dimpled cellulite fall upon the heads of all members of the House of Grandville!"

"Are you trying to be funny, or are you just drunk again? Well, listen 'may the fleas from a thousand dirty billy goats infest the arm-pits of all Nickadors as well!' Ha, ha! Not very funny either, was it?"

On that note, I moved the crotchets of time, not so bad, just shades of EGBDF, and so…. bloody well… damn and I thought they'd all changed temperaments, put a penny in my cup! What an ass am I, they just sharpened the blade on the other side, but what in pig snot is going on? Dr Ash…yes…ZZzzz…zzz…off!

Karen at last decided to look for **hidden treasure** like the Will. She decided to root around the old rock-fall on the wooded summit of the hill behind their home. It was where grandpa and her step father had sexually abused her, from the age of eleven to seventeen. She had covered all the approaches, poked into every badger's set, ferreted down rabbit holes, smoked out foxes' dens, all to no purpose. But she asked herself for the hundredth time, would he have hidden it in that place of torture? Would he have secreted it there because he knew the place had curse on it and that Karen shunned the spot? She pushed her way through the underbrush along the overgrown pathway, moving forward, her arms outstretched, her fingers curled, her garden trowel at the ready. It was two hours to dusk, two hours for her to make the final frenetic effort. She looked sat the outcrop of rocks leading up to the moist green area where she had been such a willing, bewildered, branded victim for so long, how she hated them now, she couldn't even stand hearing their names, - but these horrific reflections were drowned out by the thought of the large amounts of cash almost in her hands, via the will - no, the bloody bastard Pa, could not cut her off, nor her Ma, nor or her sister, dirty Julie and her useless Dishcloth, money which guaranteed her escape from the two most hated and feared men in her life, one dying, one dead, with clown Nickador a stranger in a stranger land, a walking-dead witness to her little hell on earth. Nickador was going nowhere too! She would make it if no one else would, and the family church would applaud. Yes. Make it! Now, now, now! Yes, she moaned to the skies, "Give me the slugs that crawl under the ivy to any of them any day!" She would show them. With a brain raging with pictures of wealth and liberty, revenge and thousands of Nubian lovers, she pressed on. She thrust her hands into a pile of blackened ash leaves and encountered something soft below, something that was not in the texture of wet rotting foliage. She saw she held in her hands the canvas ground-sheet of a back-packer, the pack, covered with leaves and moss, already half open, surely a propitious sign! With a snarl of triumph, she dragged the top open, and began tearing out a mass of printed material, some contained in plastic covers, others open to the clotted soil, but all in readable condition. "Just the will, just the will!" she panted, as she plucked out yet more material from it. She recoiled at the sudden, glutinous, stink as new stuff hit the ground, exposed…a pile of sex magazines, all with fornicating groups on the front, in all positions on the inside, "no!" she muttered through clenched teeth! - she had located the damnable perverts' secret porn mine! She yelped in rage. She groped below the lurid yellowed pages. There was still room for the Will. Underneath, she made out in the fading light, an obscene jumble of sex toys - pink, black, yellow and purple multi-phallused dildos, she gasped in delight and disappointment - 'Reel Feels, Arse Plugs, Giant 12 inch Twister-Sister-Sets, Cock Rings, Black -Shafted Clit- Stims, Tingling Tubes, Pulsating Fists, Anal Bullets, Spunk Jetters, Gel and Pussy Probes, Slippery Lickers, Buzzcock Masseurs…' all unwashed and giving off a foul stench of crotch and minge. In blind rage, she raised the trowel over the obscene pile. Her weapon bounced off the rubbery fleshy genitalia, crushing phalluses, smashing arse bullets, cock rings, the 'Twister Sisters' punctured beyond redemption; the Tubes and Probes and Fists and fiddles, fractured and ripped into pieces by the force of her assault. Childhood nightmare images flared in her mind, mixing with this unholy pink hell, now covered with the technicolour pages of the flapping magazines. She slashed and raged and stamped them back into the damp vile Pa and Granpa hole where all the shit really belonged. With a wild, final kick and a scream to frighten the squirrels, she saw she was now back where she had started, jobless, homeless, penniless, with a walking dead reject for a partner and a cannibalistic family, – and in front of her, her whole life summed up, a scatter of nauseating sex toys and squirming earth worms! She retched emptily at the pink stink and collapsed amid the abused erotic paraphernalia, burying her head in her hands. She did not stop weeping until the sun rose.

A flood of unnamed repulsive portraits is now among us, were they ever tiny tots, the devils, on the short hill tops?......go...look...an ask... Nickador observed **the Levitation Man,** an OAP, or seriously sturdy skeleton, male, hanging onto a lamp-post at the bus-stop by the lake.

"You OK, sir?" I ask.

"You wouldn't have a book on levitation, would you?"

"Sorry, I don't have anything on levitation."

"'Cos if I knew how to levitate I could float up from this lamp-post as if I had wings and float away from all the crap down below here."

"Tell you what – give me your name and address, and if I ever find a really good book on levitation, I'll send it on to you. I promise."

"Ta, mate, made my day! Oops, nearly went that time!"

I paused at a bench, call Dr Ash, to focus on the usual sliding slices of darkness, again for everyone…the scene is arranging itself… in Ma's apartment yesterday after the Clinic, looked me up and down and said I had **no decent clothes**. Listen. She pointed at my crotch, "That light flannel material, shows up the stains, see, all yellowish, wash afterwards, and wear heavier trousers, a tweed, it's not so noticeable, you can't go into a classroom like that, too embarrassing. People will talk. Here's some money, buy a new pair of trousers with thicker flies on your way back."

Humbled by my own urine, cash in hand, I realized that even my poor piss-stains were not beyond my in-law's tender mercies. Avalanches on the whole lot of them and their execrable dual units called marriage, the lying, rotting, selfish, toxic, syphilitic, plotting cells of hissing vipers!

So I say, but what to do, Dr Ash? Tell all. I want to be caparisoned and chain-mailed in a furious charge on the terrified front ranks of the putrid Bourgeois banking cavalry!

Zzzz, Zzzz, Zzzz... the... here? I shake awake to the tragedy of **the School bus**, another comedy for the Grandvilles. "Crane on building site topples onto passing school bus, many students perish," declared their class teacher reading from the local paper's headlines. "Here is the list of the dead: students Hung Chew, Prudence Levellis Vosper, Petrea Noye, Nasir Damit, Maine Juniper, Hercule Voise, Wendy Gude, Uriel Moons and lastly, but not leastly, Theodoric Hyacinthus." He looked around. "Anyone else here absent?" he queried with a grin, then roared with laughter. What a joker! Ha, ha, ha! Ho, ho, ho!

A single solitary scream comes from the old torture chambers of Torquemada all over the place...the plain-chanting of distant fiendish holy subject matters and priestly nomenclatures... bloody silly protestors, the wrack, for example, fact of life, still with us...I slip off ...God bless all their poor souls...

Grandpa and a Villa...well, it's grand old grandpa again, the kick-shitter, kidshagger of the boulevard, this time, just a few sordid seconds, whatta laugh, ha, ha, ha! the utterly respected, immeasurably wealthy , grizzled old tyrannical billy- goat, they said, ho, ho, ho! bought this villa on the coast of Apulia in southern Italy. His did this so he could avoid tax in his own proud nation. When he arrived for his first holiday, he immediately put up a spiked fence of iron railings around the property, "keep out the foreign beggars," he said. After his first week, he put his washing out to dry, on the railings of course, two pairs of old socks, three pairs of underpants and five handkerchiefs - 'which grimy articles of clothing,' his neighbours asserted, 'kept away the mendicants' 'but they swore, 'the railings kept out nothing.' One night, the whole first wash disappeared in one swell foop. The railings next, from the roots, so it was soon just the same old blank sandy space in front of the villa, and finally the walls of the villa began to go, brick by dusty brick, too. He had nowhere to lay his crooked, scabby head, so he sold the whole lot to the nearest bidder, the local brothel Madame, girded up his filthy loins, pulled up his bulging trousers, put on his pongy trainers and did a runner, never to return. Ha, ha, ha! Ho, ho, ho! Bad old grandpa, what a laugh… old pong machine… him and his girls, makes you laugh, not the girls though…Chitti, there you are, or are not, come in to my little vision, most welcome, are you as a whisper in a shadow in a cave, like the bat, the friendliest ghost in flitting Christendom and elsewhere, comrade, guardian, mate to all elephant lovers…well… **Clock in quick, Chitti**, launch the word!

"Sorting it out! Got it! Listen! You, the best teacher I ever had, Master Nickador: **"**Nevertheless, there must be Leaders to take care of these probably dangerous children, and there are leaders of many sorts - cruel ones, gentle ones, big, small and rare ones, so many it ends in total puzzlement. But the word 'dictator' now comes in to the business, with its awful brother 'corruption.' Let us look briefly at dictators, ones who have benevolence in them, those who will sacrifice themselves for their dangerous children, guide them, feed them, educate and chastise them, and keep the safe from snares and traps and treacheries of the world. These Leaders will teach the children so hard that they will never have enough time to make trouble. The people will become so educated they will invent their own systems of knowledge, so they can become their own servants as well as leaders. They are free. The bad dictators simply do the opposite. When they do, both dictatorship and democracy can be blown to pieces. I speak from the heart – of Bangkok…and my tottering self, like yours….is… "

Chitti Magayathon, thanks from all of me for all of you, always, for never being truly political! A true comrade in the absence of comradeship is a true comrade…or I think so… Zip to…. **Dr Ash talks of symptoms**… the buzzerbuzzes, from somewhere at home, roll of shiters, really, I think. I anwered the phone inside the ache inside my head. Dr Ash, Shame—of-it-All, mate, doctorate magnificent in Biology! bass guitarist in harmony, and one who warned me to go there, Manorbier, Minervia - long shots away……fine, thanks. Yes, no one here, yet. Ref the symptoms…I did give you the list… more samples…how?…"facial buds…paper cups, cigarette ends…" OK. No, as before…fever, turning a light green colour, speaks but garbled, hides everything even his bed-pan, gives the nurses a laugh…fits, fevers and convulsions I said but all mild the Clinic doc said, Dr Klein, in Pa's back pocket… funds galore…for what I know not, at least not yet…… no, in food, on food, salt cellars, from human hand, lots out of herbal borders as you said, Dan, I followed your traces, it seems to all fit…. And your last query, where was Pa when he collapsed? Answer, tending the bar-b-q with a long fork, his own JFK imitation, fresh chicken wings, just lit, yes, fire wood, Pa cut it up, his own wood-cutter as well, no charcoal… pillars of smoke, still green, the fool, tyrant Pa couldn't light a matchstick. Who else? just the two ugly sisters, in and out, and mostly Ma, sprinkling the pork chops with oregano…no not Doctor Klein, he left early. Who do I think? Where the money is, follow the greed I'd say? Got my hands full, on the brink, his last legs, and I'm no expert…and no Will in sight…god, how they're sweating, in every crook and nanny, not a legal document this side of paradise…I'll be OK, if you could just give the stuff I sent the quick once over and let me know your findings... yes, temperature, pulse…as good as done…all in my notes…tons of flowers, ointments - what? Yes, azaleas, or was it oleanders, on his bedside table…to show how much he was loved, of course, instructions at the bottom of the bed…don't know what I'm quite involved in…sneak in when I take Julie, and now Ma as well, in her new garb as guardian angel!... well, I'd say, the old hag, a real whirl there, now she's all but boss, two lesser harpies, Karen, my slut, and Julie her sorority side-kick, another called 'Dishcloth' who supplies the family with hash, including Pa, just, Grandpa on cloud 99, thank god, fornicating with the earth worms, no doubt, Grandpa who was high as a kite most of the time in his distinguee years…girls turned up swearing he was fun but sharpened all the bar-b-q cutlery in an exemplary fashion, no kiddings….yes, all for his farewell…the timetables, signed by Klein, too, bowel lavage, alimentary enema, the usual, as you outlined, Dan, done. What!? a little teaching job! - never mind if it's just 'supply,' a few hours to start!...that'll do fine… take the away train… ta, ta …. for the whole lot, Dr Ash, some voices are always welcome and you are one, now to the next…blanks filled in, like graves, don't you worry… cheers and cheers…back soon…but first – **The Firing of Nickador…**

…the Director, all six foot six of him, rose from his desk, smoothed down his mane of blond hair, narrowed his hard eyes and motioned for Nickador to sit down. Nickador had been wondering all day. Was his temporary contract under review now? Was this an extension? A rejection? Not a hint had come from the Director's office. He liked to watch members of his staff shitting themselves in front of him. An extension?'! Anything less was would be a disaster. His work permit was still going through, his bank balance, not balancing; marriage on the brink, rent due and he needed socks, underpants, a fresh crotch, change of urine, loose change for the public telephone, a new was suit out of the question. He was in his working hacking jacket, the only one around. Nickador looked at his boss as if he was the most benign man in the world; the hulking boss gave a glacial smile, and narrowed his eyes again, how he hated the sunshine, especially in his office; the Director brooded for a second, then with a spread of his hands, and a toss of the leonine head, proclaimed, "There is no place for you here now. I know how difficult it is for you, with a new wife, too, I believe, that you can't afford the essentials yet, but the documentation is not looking good, I know it is only a few days before the end of term and salary payments cease then, so you'll have to hurry to come to a decision. He paused, seemingly taken aback by Nickador's lack of response, "we all know you come from a distant family, nothing to be ashamed of, but you will have a problem later in life when you have to explain your absence of success to your children. Children can be very unforgiving, as remorseless as any wife. Now my advice is, speak to her of her your situation here and now, no frills, no excuses, women can always tell, so she'll be prepared for the coming difficult circumstances. She is also looking for a job, I understand, but what about yourself, got to have a woman look up to you, without respect you are lost, they will not stand by you. So, be determined! Get up, get out, out! Push! Push! you'll never get anywhere by just sitting back and dreaming of good jobs and social success. And you can forget your paper on Exhortation to Intellectualism, you don't need to get published any longer, Intellectualism is not a forte now. So, Nickador, you are off our staff complement as from now..." again he stopped and looked keenly at his prey. Was Nickador holding back. Did he have contacts he, the boss, knew nothing of? He relaxed and tried to sound reassuring, more to himself, it seemed, than anyone else. "But I'll tell you what, I'll put your name down on our internal County Education list for temporary teachers, informal info for us Directors, learn a lot from supply teaching you know, get to recognise the lay of the land, so to speak. The emended list will circulate during the coming holiday, but I can't promise anything. It doesn't matter if people see you are out of a job, and gossip of course, which won't please your wife, but many of us have been through this procedure. Bracing! No? Well, if you..." He waited for a reaction but Nickador merely held out his hand. The Director fell momentarily silent. Had he screwed Nickador hard enough? Difficult to tell when your victim is the silent type from far away. The Director finally deigned to shake the extended hand.

"Yes, one does learn a lot from supply teaching, sir."

"Well, I'm glad you're taking it this way. I'm sure you'll make a fine teacher one day. And regards to your wife. Good morning er...Nickador –'god, what a silly name!' he muttered as the oddly christened reject turned away.

"The family will be happy," Nickador smiled to himself. The sun was shining directly overhead. Fine! He didn't look back. Nickador had definitely left the building.

Nickador hurried home. He had to send his **'Exhortation to Intellectualism**,' a paper the Director had strictly instructed him to prepare for publication, an essential part of his career here as a pedagogue, he had been told. He glanced through the pages, yes fine, it had lost none of its pretentiousness, ignorance, pomposity and dogmatism, perfect present teacher stuff! He blew his nose and read out: 'just to declare at the outset, that I respect all discarded arts installations for they represent double the original art creation, the rejected and the accepted' – (and ain't no silver-backed bouncer gonna change my mind, babee!) Pardon me there! 'Dangling fruit and loom patterns are still champion and ever appear in the wig-wams of Pocohontas and her designing braves. See the tapestries! Later, in time, wind-blasted concrete ruins rose up as circular as any of the Macdonald Towers among the Gardens of Mild Regurgitation, of ours. Ignore the Saxon dog-pooos - those malodorous striations will be forever melted in the typhoons of the coming mind. Why, you might as well try to re-build the pyramids themselves with pebble-dash stone-cladding resistant to all-weather shopping. God bless those lost ubermarkets I say! I remember with affection the great Potseen Chambers of Antrim which, with tall bluish spun-glass Porter beakers everywhere, served ham and eggs to the initiate all day. Ta to Ma, Patrick! The homeless Monk who still wonders the back alleys of Aberystwyth, unrecognised and unrecorded, is even now tempted by our rosy-hued alcopops and the scattered chicken bones of KFK, with undigested morsels still hanging off, daily, like bloody stripped boarskins. But not to worry, the plague of fleas worrying the part-time college servers will be decimated by our flocks of domesticated pigeons at the source, it's well known. Relax afterwards on our golf-driving ranges, our long summer outlet evenings, go crazy with your Warehouse stamps, knock on the heavy oak doors of your Bank Overdraught for that fiftieth ruinous loan at all costs! And above everything – intellectualise!! - it does not matter what, as long as no one understands it, the best people pretend to, which is good enough for most of us! Once inside, ignore the open floors, the weeded ceilings, the decaying dividends, the collapsed planks of the gold-toothed vaults, the lost chambers of commerce, yes, shoot out all the security lights with your cheese-gun and have a ball – these are tomb-tingling times! Intellectualise, mes braves! Intellectualise, this is my new Exhortation! And I am off to taste some of it right away! Lucifer bless you Monsieur le Directeur, I shall ponder to the end! Ugh, ugh! Ugh! What a truly loathsome pile of bile you are! And zzz zzz zzz avalanches on the lot of you! Zzzzzzzz...a looming flight now...Zzz...in the green distances, the tiny pebbles rolled on to sand, till the onrush turned and the spumed flesh was worn to whispers even now as he slept on, deep and whissssp...zzz zzzz into the Immemorial spirit of service to the Muse, a heart-loving icon rises... Yes! - **St David (aka 'Minervia')** the son of Princess

Non who gave birth to him on the edge of a cliff in a thunder storm. The promontory on which it stood thrust out into the Atlantic before a vast oceanic horizon, endless and terminal. Minervia's Cathedral (the nave built by Gerald the Welshman) is a place of miracles – didn't the floor with it encaustic medieval tiles, rise up at the back so the congregation could see their 'Minervia' with a dove on his shoulder, revealing the True Word, before departing upwards ushered by flocks of angels and the sound of heavenly choruses. His final words "Do the little things, be joyful…" were heard and sung by everyone. So holy was he, two pilgrimages to Minervia's altar were worth one to Jerusalem, Jesus! as popular as Christ's sepulchre itself! Today the benches are full of worshippers come to honour a son of Dewsland, a warrior, a scholar Nickador's dear Dad, a herald of the whole of humanity, bless him, bless Minervia-Dafydd too, who granted him one or two of the outstanding decorations of life!

The Cathedral rose up in the centre of a walled 'city' the size of six football pitches, situated in a huge dip in the ground due to an unearthly earthquake which made the West End lean outwards. This persuaded the masons and planners to construct a painted camber-beam roof which could bend with the earth-shifts and not tumble down. On the joints of the beams were carved a variety of heads from saints to cupids. Far below on the underside of the misericorde seats were more carved heads, principally of the Green Man who was said to reside in the copses on the periphery of the sacred terrain. In Minervia's sanctuary, Abraham's Stone looks down on the kneeling pilgrims, a holy relic indeed! The floor, as is well known and most noticeable, slopes from east to west, with one end higher than the other, sometimes known as Minervia's holy tilt, 'holy' due to virtual survival of all natural shocks as well as the depradations of the alien Saxon, not to mention the savage Viking swinish-invaders. Due to the urgings of the local saints, Alfred of the Cakes begged Minervia to civilize the greedy new arrivals. And Minervia did, and behold, the pagan Saxon was cleansed by the holy spirit and lived in peace until the nastier Norman anti-Christians conquered all. In the perpetual Spring of the shaded dells in the grounds outside, ten thousand bunches of Tenby daffodils glow in the sunshine so the whole east side of the edifice shimmers like a golden palace, the brilliant glassy windows adding to the incorporeal luminescence, a supernatural geometry where 'bare ruined choirs' are said to be break into song when St David-Minervia rises to preach every Xmas Day as he has done for over two thousand years...I say...the holy book and the... scriptures and Gerald... zzzz...is it...? the sands of...what really?....zzz...zzz... wake not...no...

Karen finally spotted her husband by the pool in the western copse, under the weeping willow looking up through the light green feathery boughs to the cerulean reaching heavens, yes, gazing into the infinite again, a bad sign for any lady-girl-partners in the offing. She strode across the greensward, stopped, crouched, clutching the front of her panties, and yelled over the daffodils, "For fuck's sake, aren't there any bloody toilets in this fucking place?"

He groaned profoundly as the skin of recollection burst precisely parallel again…in the sitting room of the family's skiing flat in the mountains, **Karen again** screamed at her sister, "You disgust me, whatever you say. You did sleep with your grotty pick-up in my own bed. One night stand! A casual fuck, like two dogs! You did! All night long, I could hear you grunting like a pig! In my bed! And I was on the sofa."

"So what!" shot back Julie, "you had sex with the concierge on that sofa when the parents were in their own bedroom there, slut!"

"You'd fuck with an ant-eater, you nymphomaniac!"

"Nymphomaniac yourself, you fuck with OAP's."

"So did you!"

"Not that I really needed it, bitch, it was just for fun!"

"Don't come all morality with me!"

They raged at each other as if everybody else,

including himself, were invisible. Nick went for a short visit to the toilet, his usual retreat up here for a bit of peace and quiet.

"Slut, yourself …" came the usual riposte. "And what about 'Dishcloth?' You were unfaithful to him."

"Don't make me laugh, just as long as he tends his plants, he'll do as he's told."

"And why did Ma give you that whole lobster?"

"It was for both of us…"

"If you two are up to..."

"…nothing, Ma's getting old, that's all."

"Well, when Pa's gone, she'll be boss…"

"…and Jesus, does she know it."

"Got to keep a close eye on her. Both of us."

"Both of us," Julie repeated, calming down.

" Perhaps he'll have another epileptic fit…"

"…I don't trust that Doctor…"

"…we can work it out, half way there…"

"Damn his soul! **Pa hides his money**, conceals his Will…on purpose!"

"We'll find it, not going to rob me!"

"It's that medicine of Dr Klein's…"

"…Dr Klein's knows his job, don't you worry. He also knows which side his bread is buttered on. And don't try to get him into bed either."

"Is that all you think of?"

"You slept with grandfather!"

"Shut the fuck…up!"

They were face to face when Nick came out to see what was going on, then hair to hair, then violently wrestling head to head on the floor.

Nickador picked up the bottle of brandy on the sideboard, went onto the balcony and began drinking at the small table there. The battle raged on, as usual. 'Remy Martin,' very good, he thought, as he settled down in the warm wicker arm-chair. He barely followed the screams of insults. If half were true, both sisters were for the cells, and their matronly Ma and highly respected

Pa, too.

He was in a pleasant alcoholic doze when Karen banged open the veranda door and roughly shook him awake.

"Snore!? Is that all you can do?"

"I beg your pardon…" Nickador managed.

"…you just walz in here as if you owned the place, leave me with that dirty thing, Julie's gone mad, breaking up the place, and you just run out here and get drunk on Ma's best brandy…things are going on, and you can't see!"

A crash of breaking crockery came from the kitchen, "for God's sake help me, she's still at it!" She snatched the empty bottle and waved it under his nose. "Is this all you can do when I need your fucking help? Is it?"

It all passed over his head, good old Remy, you could always rely on him…twinkle, twinkle…zzz…zzz… zzz…

Chitti floats past on a raft of bamboo frames, loaded with houris and mangoes and Columbian white, the fodder of fools, and the statues of the big fat Buddhas, bless them, my dear Chitti sails in a boat of reeds far sturdier than mine…"hey, Chitti buddy, row on! The illuminations are coming! Forward!!" Chitti did so. "Thank you Chief Chitti Magayathon, never too late mate, always comrade, fresh from Bangkok's thousand days of stellar enlightenment, where your smiling spirit ever holds sway!"

Chitti: "Now hearken, mate - Nevertheless, there must be Leaders to take care of these probably dangerous children, and there are leaders of many sorts - cruel ones, gentle ones, big, small and rare ones, so many it ends in total puzzlement. But the word 'dictator' now comes into the business, with its awful brother 'corruption.' Let us look briefly at the leaders, ones who have benevolence in them, those who will sacrifice themselves for their dangerous children, guide them, feed them, educate and chastise them, and keep the safe from snares and traps and treacheries of the world. These Leaders will teach the children so hard that they will never have enough time to make trouble. The people will become so educated they will invent their own systems of knowledge, so they can become their own servants as well as their own leaders. They are free. The bad dictators simply do the opposite. When they do, dictatorships will be blown to pieces!"

"No doubt of it, my Chitti late mate, nature as well as nurture, bites back! I wave, you wave, all from so long ago, but that 'ago' is long enough and deep enough, 'love,' it's called."

"Cheers and cheerio!"

Sighs deep and long or short as one single human life, now and then whsssp...zzzz...zzzz...loves another... twinkle, twinkle...

The warbling Gate-Keepers of the Wasteland do not go Home. Nickador entered the four foul domestic acres of the junk-space of the discarded technopolis near his home territory! Onwards he promenaded, greeting every sight with a groan; the landfill park was scattered with discarded claw—hammers this time, the line of welded containers on the western side had become adopted homes; something crunchy, rusty and new every time! - the tumbledown industrial treasuries went on and on - follow the toxic mayonnaise, folks! the oily over-spills, the fly-tipped sofas, the flattened coffee filters, still percolating among the cockroaches, the ubiquitous oxidised sewage exits, the acrid bubbling chemical compounds; phlegm-coloured leach oozing from collapsed mole-holes; onwards over square yards of splintered glass and bashed brickbats all the way; over the splintered boards of the rotted 'executive pavilion,' long expired, the smashed wash-basins with their yellowed toilet bowls, the crumbled, plugged up cellars; the scorched tumbledown chimneys, ovens gaping like starving steel; the seized-up pulleys rusting in the iron rafters; the old railroad with granite chippings still intact; piles of cut-up cross-hatch barbed wire; small bunkers, with iron doors hanging open, sleeping place for foxes, storage space for rodents; a pigeon-loft lying on its side; a scrubland of soggy, raw earth flooded with clinker, slag and sludge lagoons. He came to a halt in front of a brand new hot water copper cylinder; he kicked it, it responded hollowly; yes, he was close to home alright. (Not to mention the people!) But where, he wondered in this steel-works nightmare, were the tender floral tributes of yesteryear? Crested toads were now beginning to inhabit his infant Garden of Eden - he told the world and the world spun away indifferently! Where had the greater honey-guide wrens gone, he insisted, the common darters, the four-spotted chasers, the black-tailed-skimmer-dragon-flies, the lesser grasshopper warblers, the yellow ragwort, the wild carrots, the crozier bracken and the curling bindweed everywhere? Where had all these perfumed bunches of delight gone?! And where their homes, - the dens, the dells, the copses, the dingles? Wherever, he had done right, the boy, to piss off to fairer climes, bigger roasts, more frequent cash oases! He had beheld the Wasted Land of his Fathers, what an age, what a homecoming! He brushed away a brief tear. Onwards to Avallon, then, ye warbling gate-keepers of Cymru, the only way left for 'Hendre'! He reclined on a sofa somewhere and lo and behold, breathless again, **after the funeral** he soon had a dream about an anonymous coffin with a stranger in it. As he stared, the screws unscrewed themselves and dropped to the floor. The lid slid off, revealing the corpse of the suicide, a man of boundless self-centredness and uncontrollable gluttony, some charisma, babee! His widow's last words to him were, "You're in a hell of a hole, Horace, love, now pull yourself out of it, you fat slug!" and then had allowed her Pekanese to crap on the front wheel of the hearse. Somehow she had neglected to inform his 'friends' of the unfortunate demise of her man, so the few mourners who had discovered the death by pure coincidence, wondered around the half deserted chapel, trying to find ushers, or simply other mourners to pretend to grieve with. The coffin was draped with gray gauze, with a few drooping bouquets on top. The suicide, for it was he, one of those sad Cherrymen. Whose, you ask? Everybody's! During his last moments the suicide had surrounded himself with photos of his mother, from babyhood to manhood, Mr Near-Death, of Harriet's kith and kindle, and planted a kiss on each one in the photo, then swallowed a number of seriously large sleeping pills and emptied a seven-year-matured bottle of Glenlivet, and launched the first and last second of his poor blasted, unblessed, untoasted life, and then had sloped off to join all the others in the Land of Rope, and Glory, somewhere... wheresoever, whomsoever directs …

"Fucking Harriet should have found her own bloody man like that", hissed Karen, "teach the cow a lesson."

The widow carried a small wreath of flowers, with many Lilies of the Valley, of her own choosing, flowers which would best express her own inconsolable grief; her porcine features turned a raw pink as she dabbed the tears flowing down her cheeks with an inch-square silk hanky and clung sobbing to the arm of her latest lover. This was to be her day! They were shown into the chapel. The priest of the diocese wandered into view, still pulling on his surplice. He glanced at the front pews, "hello," he said to the seated figures. They ignored him. "Are you family?" Karen merely raised her eyebrows. This was enough for the man of God. "God welcome you," he intoned on - and thought he had never had a nuttier bunch of mourners before, "The deceased was a fine Christian…" he had to say something – "are you brother or sister?" Karen merely shrugged. "This man of god was so pious, such a Christian, I would often find him here in front of the high altar, on his hands and knees, begging forgiveness for his multitudinous sins and many turpitudes, such humility! He was loved by his family and respected by his neighbours, however few, however rare, they were precious to him." The priest made a hasty sign of the cross over Karen, who promptly recoiled, hissing, "Nooooo!" the holy man pressed on hopelessly, "this man believed in the after life and in the life before too. Bless you, Corpse, as you join your larger family of corpses," he paused, aside, "cancel that, it's the grief of the occasion. I did not mean it. Thank you. Amen." he pulled his surplice closer to him. A congregation of mediaeval imps and diableries alright. Most of the lost, spare congregation had now wandered off. This man of God did not deign to bless their going any more. The widow however, stumbled to the edge of the grave, and was only saved by her new boy-fried from following the flowers inside. She gripped her fists, sank to her knees, and shrieked silently to her deeply repugnant inner self ' – 'the bastard is dead! All men are dead, dead Jailors. I am free!" She clung icy-eyed to her beau, he was a great fuck. Ahhhrrghh, she growled. The last of the mourners petered out without a smile, leaving her well alone, spitting blood. All this on her 20th wedding anniversary. The priest noted through all the solemn ceremonies, that no one had wiped the dog turd off the wheel of the hearse, at least not to his knowledge. Where in the hell did the crap come from, he asked, puzzled, there wasn't a dog in sight. What was happening? What was going on in his own graveyard? He flopped onto the square laundered high altar, like a discarded harvest offering and….Zzzzz, Zzzzz…

"Nickador, lad, Nicky, wake to the bees! Go, go, go! Buzz, buzz…"

As well as the somnolent priest, Nickador slept till nightfall. Dr Ash alerted him, as per usual the sly non-stop sentinel! The procession of his mate Pete's **farewell ceremony** called him over. Nickador was there in an instant. It was 'along the margin of a lake, beneath the trees' they walked and talked in the bright Spring breeze. Two magpies flew across their path and disappeared into the leafy sycamores, always in pairs the Magpies, never separated except in death. Pete had christened the spot after the faithful birds, the 'Two Magpies.' My old army pal, Pete, was in good walking and warbling form. He had on his climbing boots from the Royal Engineers, scuffed and ripped, now a purplish-khaki hue, up hill to John O'Groats, down hill to Land's End, he'd marched the latest Everest trek. We had known each other from the day of the Troop Intake on the military train at Liverpool Pool Street Station, on Sept 23rd of that decade, when they both set out for the horrific khaki-and-drill new world – without their permission of course. Pete was the embodiment of human kindness. He was the most popular man he'd ever met, beloved by all. He was also the fittest, a mountain climber, parachutist, deep sea diver, athlete and regimental squash champion, among other activities. His bailouts of friends were legendary. He stopped at the little inlet, where the boulders grew big and round and smooth, with green lichens gleaming in the sun. They sat on the damp seats and continued their colloquy. In another second, Nick saw them, even then, and fifty years later, as old codger OAP's, resting like now, talking about something or nothing but revelling in the heart-warming friendships of youth in old age. They would never run out of reflections, observations, insights and implosions of understanding, however banal - friends, mates, buddies, they would reach the heights of doom and the depths of hilarity, why not? - they were true 'comrades of war', the elite, survivors of every shitty hostile Front, with croaking laughter in the van! Pete had bought a small cottage in this place, his delightful '**Two Magpies**' and came for a run past this spot every dawning.

Nick slapped his chest. "Hear that, Pete? That's an A1 health echo! There's irony for you! Just had my annual check up, Doc gave me a clean bill, told me just to keep doing whatever I'm doing now, chats, I swear, lakes and sycamores, magpies, pints at the end of the odd day, and do it all over again! You had your check up yet, Pete?" Pete pointed at the black sedan which was driving past on the other side of the hedge, "I swear that machine's been following us... who...is it!? ... is it..? ... Look! Nick! Look!" But when Nick looked, there was no one in sight.

"Well, have you, Pete?"

"What?"

"Had a check up,

"Why? I'm not sick."

"Only takes five minutes."

"No." he grunted, one of the few times I'd seen Pete short-tempered.

"Well..." I began, "...no, do not!" he interrupted, extremely irritated. I picked up a flat stone and skimmed it across the smooth waters, "I hope we both will still be doing this, Pete, when we're seventy four. That is all.

Your throw first! " Pete threw and Pete won, his stone skipped ten times, Nick's only four.

Nick got the call not much later from a visiting mutual friend at Pete's cottage. "Is that you, Nick? Look, get ready, **very bad news**." His blood turned to ice. "It's Pete, he's…dead. This morning, Doc's just left. His brother's here, in that stupid black saloon of his, parked outside, just 'dropped in on the off chance'. Yes, massive heart attack, brought on by stresses and strains over the years, Doc said, all that climbing and stuff. His boots still by the back door, ready to go. Doc said he was dead before he hit the ground, didn't know a thing ….where? On the path, by the lake, out for a run, that little inlet with boulders. Yes, yes, that's the place….he mentioned…I hadn't been there for years…the 'Two Magpies…' yes…" 'Hey, Dr Ash, don't keep still going, quick, fade, a massive one, to not think it out…Pete, Pete. Pete, with whom he'd drunk orange squash laced with Vodka on many a working afternoon, especially when they went to the cinema when the pubs were shut, 'Rock Around the Clock!…' Pete, not Pete, yes, Pete… for God's sake, Dr Ash, **cut to Chitti smiling,** whatever the conditions, whatever the abjects. Go, go, go ChittiI. Chitti was there in a mini-second to do his best on the podium of fucking life I suppose. Pal Chitti warbled at once, "To control the country we now have a new system called 'democracy.' Democracy is government always by the people. In this way, the government and governors are the servants of the people and are given occupations by the people. The people will allow the employees to occupy their jobs as long as the job pleases the state of being employed. In this case the people must be cunning enough to practice control of their employees. It the people are too weak and no good, and cannot control their employees as well as possible, the word 'chaos' will take place in this business. Goodness will explode and the end of days is in sight."

"Yes, like in the film. **Ta, Chitti**, you're confronting a recovered man with your valuable addition to the treasury of English vocabulary, I assure you, and a surprising expansion of our political understanding. All in a second! We will soon be in the town square playing bowls, I hope, and chatting the air out of the skies. So, twinkle, twinkle, hang onto those libertarian chants, they are fewer than we suppose, however much more they seem. Hi and lo, Chitti, my bestest one, with Pete also number one, my favourite chums, never give up those climbing boots! - so humble, so worn, so brave! Fade, you bums out there, you toilet-wall sisters, you pissovers, you shitesnipers, you coin-intoxicated filleted farts, fade outta sight, man, into earth's vast midden, your eternal home! - you have nothing to do with Minervian's joy and star-defying comradeshships. Never! Again the dream came, uninvited and foul… as the usual **Pillars of smoke** rose from the stunning chimneys of the local crematorium, some kind of crystal clear chaos had broken out at the Clinic. Dr Klein had just hurried back from a most lucrative Tuscan hospitalier venture and had walked, well known to himself, right into the usual shite, not unbeknownst to the rest of the sodheads, a quite organised huge dollop of spreading ordure. What was up? The dreadful progenitor, Pa, had risen from the dead! He had broken out a fire-alarm axe, had rushed out to the lawn uttering primitive samurai war-cries and stooped ready to ignite the bar-b-q, all set up by the lovely Head Nurse in advance, with charcoal briquets and twisted papers, Wall's sausages lovingly prepared by her sweet hand. Conflagration fuels, the twigs of trees , the chopped up boughs in a pile, branches of exotic shrubs and bushes as super kindling laid out under the grille. Glare-eyed Pa, hurled the axe aside, it had served its purpose, noisome to the end. He lit the pyre with a single match and as the flames whooshed upwards, a stinky-poo odour of petroleum pervaded the open air. Pa pranced around the bonfire, for that is what the al fresco luncheon had become, whooping like a Comanche Brave in mid snake-dance, pale face speak with forked tongue, and about time too! It was three of the clock when the ladies turned up as invited at that precise moment. Amazingly Dr Klein was calmness herself. He had stood there through the whole macabre athletic ceremony, smiling benignly, arms crossed, evidently enjoying the spectacle and was now ready to move but rapidly. Arms flayling, Pa piled on more of the recently felled foliage, but after a few steps was engulfed by the smoke from the greenery. He staggered back, frothing at the mouth, rubbing his eyes as if going blind, barking like a dog. His gyrations came to an abrupt halt. He massaged his now swollen belly, stiff as a plank, howling in pain, and made a dash for his old sleeping quarters. D. Klein collared him and kindly frogmarched him onwards in the right direction. Nick was honoured indeed to be able to help Dr Klein as he guided the Pa to his last twitching, writhing place of seizures, in a practically defunct state. Dr Klein at once tucked him up in his old bed, declaring the spot an Isolation Unit, with no disturbance at any cost. He strapped the gasping madman back into the narrow couch, not too tight, just so the Pa knew who was boss. Dr Klein administered a vigorous gastric lavage (pump) - yes, Dr Klein had been prepared. The Pa had been fumigated externally and now purged internally, though he knew little about it, but he had given enough cash on the spot for the good Doctor to declare his independence from Pa and Ma and flit away like a gilded butterfly to more distant climes - to perform last rites, or wrongs as the case may be! The women were not spared these ghastly scenes, being quite habituated to them, until they were ordered by Dr Klein to depart to the unsavoury luxury home of the gallant Grandvilles , and to return, if ever, on a word of command from only himself, in person. There they were also to bid farewell to the dumb-hangin'-on foreigner, Nickador, a complete surprise, the alien swarthy drip, who had managed to have a word or two for them that they were legally obliged to listen to, according to the lawyers of the deadly-nightshade Will, which no one had yet discovered, but which would be soon, and explain all.

They went in Ma's clattering car, muttering, grumbling, Karen hissing and belching with disgust, her own floppy man, Nickfuckindor, to talk to *them*, the girly galaxy of the house of Grandville? Well, anything for **the last testament,** she supposed, farting with anxiety, wondering what her Ma had been up to all this time, the treacherous overbearing, battle-axe banshee! Now came the sick climax of the Clinic's whole demise procedure, which no ordinary superman could ever contend with – the Clinic- presided over the last disintegrations of this-was-a-man – yes, Pa himself! - his penultimate symptoms - the onrush of bespattered tummy diarrhoeas by the dozen, acute vertigo, various hallucinations, mammoth twitchings, as mentioned, excessive salivations, clammy footsteps, ulcers of the gums, bleeding from the anus, numbness of the molars, deliriums everywhere and all quite hairless, a mountain of pain for such a dirty little creep, Pa, - not only bowing out but blowing up! Bravo!

There is no question that the good **Dr Klein** took the correct subsequent steps. Before the Attendants, or any kind of officiating medic, except his very own sexy Head Nurse, could get to him, he rushed Pa out of the back directly onto a clattering trolley right into the flaming chambers of the crematorium, where he burned Pa to a fucking crisp! Immolation by blossom! The juicy Head Nurse, still his faithful mistress over the years, now put into effect the highly practical financial aspects of the plan, the steaming corpse was mere bagatelle, an accessory, cash was really the hot spot for her and for the good Doctor, tons of folded lumpy spondulix tucked safely away in an embroidered yellow pillow case! The high strategic plan they now put into effect, the good doctor Klein had persuaded Pa to adhere to , the key, to have Pa himself declare himself, in writing, a 'death by assisted suicide' case - a legalistic high plains of new medicinal terms and terminations, marvellous solution, a neat and merciful outcome, from the humble pyre to this blazing fire! The good doctor produced a sheaf of affidavits, certificates, summaries of evidence, learned references, even slides of the creepy stuff, in crystal form, which had eventually foully done for Pa. There was little doubt that Pa, with some considerate help, had topped himself with poisons lurking in the instrument dishes and disinfected cabinets of Klein's own bloody surgery. To make 'assisted suicide' guaranteed absolutely genuine, Pa had donated half a million to the new rising Clinic in the hills of Tuscany and the slithering foxy Pa had also left sufficiently powerful legal instruments, again duly sworn, to obviate the ladies' liking for vicious confrontations, and acerbic or abrasive humours, which would lead to Pa's goods and chattels being distributed among the poor of the slums of Geneva. This shut their gobs - even wiped the greedy sneer off Ma's face for a second or two, between gulps of cut-price sea-food. This paper work exonerated all the guilty ones from any even suspicion of wrong doing, ever. An autopsy and any second opinion, was out of the question, cos, man, the man was toast. Ma, the Misses,

Julie and Kate were exonerated on the spot. The papers proved it beyond reason. The lady- girl-female mourners arrived at the festering apartment weeping piteously, tears of pure relief, but for the girls, there was a nasty sting to the end of it, even though all the documents had been duly signed, legitimising every dodgy infraction - why the ladies were poisoning Pa even as he was giving them permission to do it' He even joined in with a few voluntary sniffs himself. But first, dear Doctor Ash, let me say, we do act with one voice, don't we? Good! I knew you could be trusted with all the lying claptrap and phony confessionals going on all over. Yes, there were toxic substances everywhere in the environment too, dropping like the gentle dew from heaven, you knew all that mortal stuff, they had it all tied up, the lethal gals, with you as their ultimate hidden avenging angel, what a sweet little trap, I heard it all on the grapevine from the Concierge's cupboard. And you even wrote a sweet melody on the bass guitar for you and me, **'No shame at all,'**and all the other few 'I's out there in the bottomless razor-sharp crevices of life. Ta, Dr Ash, quiet exterminator of the sheer turpitudes of the normal and the abnormal too. 'O, No shame at all!' Music to my ears!

As the usual pillars of smoke rose in the distance from the wonderful chimneys of absolutely full recall, Nickador was moved to another half-smile at the ever-present farces of truth everywhere, at the same time passing on these lavish, long-winded, newly-learned wisdoms to the forever looming silhouette of the ubiquitous, approving Dr Ash, a Prime Collector, a First Mover of Harmonic Scales, a Bard out of the People of Daana, a Sir Tom Tell Truth to the end, high fives to the man who never sleeps for he has a wonderful world to keep very, very clean! Shit, who said that!?

"Hey, listen, Doc! I leapt in. I was with those beastly old hags in their fell luxury cage at the end! How I told them! I'd rumbled the Queen Bitch and the atrocious bastards of her ferocious family, which included myself, of course, and I did do it on purpose! I had all the conspiratorial snoopings in their diaries laid out in functioning blocks of irrefutable evidence, lots of ta's to you, my great reminder buddy, Dr Ash, you enlightened me! And the scratchy vocals, the interminable, incriminating regurgitations through the front door, recorded intimately on my recorder, the sweaty sisters, wrestlers of the vicious, immense and filthy, venomous Ma, all utterly recognisable in a court of law, the dirty, deadly, twisted little anal bugs, were down in black and white and on air, wired, the oldest trick in the book, man!

Ash was on the mobile in a flash, and clearly worried. **"Shut it, Nickador!"** Ash was quiet but commanding, "pride goeth,' boy, it's not over yet, so curb your blood lust for a cold supper!" Nickador realised in a flash Dr Ash was spot on. 'Cool it, dude!' is what he meant, so Nick stood tall and taciturn in front of the panting

Valkyries , cool as a cucumber in custard, so dreamy, creamy and filling.

Fat cow Ma continued to sit at the table, finishing off her lobster with an air of aggressive innocence. She finally broke her silence as she would her wind.

"What's this?" she grunted, "I'm hearing discordant notes from A Minor to E major? – plus themes of vertigo, hallucinations, mammoth twitchings, excessive salivations, I've heard it all before, on the blackest of keys! Convulsions're old hat, and all followed by, what? – nothingness followed by nothing…So…what have you got to say, you stinky Stain- Master of Dirty Flies." The girls gasped, what was disgusting old Ma alluding to this time? was she making up for her random kindnesses with rancid, grotty lies as she went along, her usual ploy, or was she just being merciless and unfeeling as two planks?

"Not over yet," Nickador repeated this golden, laconic reminder and lapsed into a wise, surely threatening silence. "And 'Nick' please, Ma" he couldn't help adding.

"What did you say?" blared Ma. Was this alien, rank Nickador, she asked herself, one even sacked by the most incompetent educational Director in the land, a worthy antagonist after all? Perhaps she ought to have given him a wank or two, she thought, or even a blow job. Too late now. No use crying over spilt milk. So perhaps the weird foreigner Nickador was leading the first wave of the skirmishers. But how much did he know? And what else did he have cognisance of? Nicky waved a hand or two quite commandingly before their very eyes. And cont'd :

"Pa collected the wood for the bar-b-q himself. With his last ounce of strength, he chopped it all up and placed it side by side with the foliage of the dead Oleandor bloom in his room, the blossoms of which as you all well knew, are poisonous to us humans, especially after being pollinated by worker wasps, slaves of the Queen Bee. The stems, which I had split to make them last longer, gives off deadly invisible vapours which are absorbed through the skin, as you all are aware of as well."

"Codswallop!" Ma ejaculated, "slanders from overseas."

"We were not aware of anything of the kind," said Karen, stamping her foot. "I was in the toilet at the time!"

"So was I," Julie added.

"He did it," shouted Karen pointing at Dishcloth, "my knowledge of pharmaceuticals is as nothing compared with his skill with mortar and pestle!"

"You can't say that and get away with it, I promise you!" gasped Dishcloth.

"Shut it!"snapped Ma, "you dumb yokel!"

The toilet-wall sisters are singing again, thought Nickador, but not quite right on key now, OK? " Nickador was self-constraint itself. "You were all in it. You, Ma, with your drops of liquid arsenic injected into the Wall's sausages, just to make sure. If you didn't get him by bed, you'd certainly get him by board. And the great Mixer and Weigher in all this ? - why our friendly lurking Dishcloth himself! It was you!"

"I never done that!" protested Dishcloth, dripping with sweat, "I just done pot!"

Were the treacherous bitch-beasts going to tan his hide after all his discrete, hard, dedicated work at the scales in the cellar? Why, his delicous Julie had assured him that he was the real hero of the hour.

"But not only were you four fucking gladiators after Pa, you were also after me!"

"Not on your silly nelly!" Ma instantly responded, "you're a stain on anybody's conscience, body and soul! Dead or alive!"

"Don't perish that thought!" exclaimed Karen,

curving her finger-nails.

"Well, I never," Nickador grinned, "will these **grubby slanders** never end?"

"You're just an old old scum bag for one so young!" spat out Karen, now getting enraged at the calmness of Nickador.

"Didn't you, Julie, tell your sister here to get rid of me by smearing our condoms, on the inside, with a powdered white solid called hydrogen cyanide, cousin of the famous Zyclon B?"

"What a sick mind!" riposted Karen, "to drag the Nazis into this!"

"As for the Will..." began Nickador. The four conspirators stiffened all ears, "Yes, what about the Will?" hissed Karen, "where in hell is it, I looked hard enough."

"We all looked hard enough," put in Ma. "But enough of this! I have only one thing to say and it is absolute. There is still no Will, l and I am next of kin and inherit everything!"

"No, you don't!" put in Julie "yes, I do!" yelled Ma. "No, you don't!" shouted Karen back. They grappled, a trio of biting chicks, rolled onto the floor, trying to tear tufts out of each others' hair. They hung on in spite of spit all over the place, gripped hard, sank their teeth in even deeper, shook each other as crocodiles do their prey in the deeps and shallows of a Queensland river. Nickador prised them apart and jerked them upright, torn and dishevelled. They snarled each other right in the face but kept their claws retracted for the moment.

"Yes," put in Dishcloth, "where's your dignity, you women!?"

"Shut your abysmal cakehole" yelled Ma, who had had the better of the brief encounter on the carpet. Dishcloth pushed her away, "Conscienceless man killer!" He was getting obstreperous. Three instant contracts were taken out on him, the dangling, soppy pestle and mortar cretin.

"Listen, you buffoons! **As for the Will...**" - silence and heavy breathing reigned again, "its fate, you ask again and again? Well, that evil piece of satan's arsehole which lists his ill-gotten gains and tells them just where to go, have been consigned to the flames!" A chorus of anguished cries and groans. " Yes! And dear old Pa himself, he really did not take to any of you, 'scum of the earth' he once called you, after a big battle. Where? That Will was attached to the peeled bark of the boughs of the oleander in full bloom. It was in the jar on Pa's hospital bedside table for weeks, slowly doing the old goat in , until I removed it to the window sill - over two feet in distance to dissipate the lethal vapours, keep them ready for a healthier stroke of fate. Hence Pa's late and early seizures and aboriginal transports among the flames on the lawn. Vile and murderous to the last drop, he was saying chop-chop fuck-off to you all, his enviable, pitiless scabby brood. The charred remnants of his loving Will now reside in the glowing embers and tasty juices of that final bar-b-q', featuring as it did, Wall's plump but healthy sausages. Your Pa's name will go down in the Grandville family annals as 'Shameless Old ancestor - Death-by-Stomach-Pump- Syndrome …"

"…don't mention his name to me!" gasped Karen.

"Nor us!" chorused the others.

"Nothing to be ashamed of, girls and boy. Now, young sly-boots himself, youthful Dr Klein showed his hand, just once, that was all he needed."

"I am the heiress of everything!" yelled Ma, "it is inevitable."

"Hang on a bit," said Nickador, smiling. He knew Ma detested his smile, especially if it came from a quiet corner of the room.

"Dr Klein directed you all to listen to me, **the filthy foreigner** here, 'Nick' to you bums, with a few final lessons on the etiquette of poisoning and how to avoid capture after killing a parent, so listen! I will answer any question, except those which contain a kernel of the truth, clearly and without discrimination." Ma, her mood still truculent though triumphal, nonchalantly finished more lobster and looked at Nickador with an air of not guilty by the foreman of the jury, but, they all noted flinched whenever Nickador opened his mouth. So what about the inheritance, sister!?

"There was no need for an autopsy, no witness available, except ours, to verify the death. Why? Because he had just gone up in a puff of smoke, far more heated than the mere little bar bar-b-q on the greensward. The good Doctor shook a sheaf of very revealing papers right under my very nose, and said, "see here, Nickador, the official cause of death – 'assisted suicide,' yes, the futile action of yet another self-condemned Cherryman! And you all knew it was 'assisted suicide,' you low suckers, here are your signed statements giving permission for the action to be taken, in some fucking God's name, his sad demise authenticated, permitted, legalised, signed by all the members of the immediate homicidal family - just as you were poisoning him, he was writing you off! You knew it too, only thing was, where was the Will? Was a Will ever just such a piece of paper? Well, now you know. But he could still have lasted one or two more days in this vale of tears if…"

"…the Dr had no antidote, I saw him leaning over the

bed, empty–handed."

"That was no empty-handed man you saw leaning over the bed, you futile old woman. No, Ma, that was the same poison, the antidote, the same white stuff but a much bigger dose, carefully weighed out… which does act nevertheless act as an antidote in correct doses…"

"…yes, I weighed it," shouted Dishcloth with pride. "I am due for my say too."

"No stay of execution is all the stay you're due," barked Karen, spitting at him.

"What are you all talking about?" burst out Ma. "I can't believe a word of this!"

"Like the Small Pox cure, Madame, which cures its own poison by a drop of itself, again in just measure. Geddit! Ask Karen, trained in poisonous pharmaceuticals, as she is," Karen at once shook her head."Never"!

"Dishcloth?" Nickador asked. Dishcloth nodded vigorously, yes, she knew!

The noddings of Dishcloth were duly ignored but a second silent contract taken out on him. "Well," Nick continued, "which one of you delivered the coup to de grace, so to speak, the last poisoned chalice, to provoke the final delirious dash of the white rabbit to its snake-like burrow in Hades-on-the-lawn?"

"There was nothing like that. I didn't touch any antidote!" Karen asserted wildly.

"The inheritance is still all mine," cried Ma, "mine, mine and mine again!"

"Rubbishy fairy tales," cried Julie, dabbing her lying eyes.

"You chucked me out!" Kate suddenly turned on her mother.

"Can't you take a joke," responded Ma, "ha, ha, ha! - we were all in it."

"I did not give him a single glass of spiked ale," asserted Karen quite illogically.

"Never forget that I am your mother," Ma returned, turning purple with rage. "fucked by your Pa to produce you load of scums…" the sisters hissed and moved to strike. Ma changed her target instantly, "And as for you, Nicafuckin'dor, there is no Will. You said so yourself. See, there is no Will!"

"There is now?" Nickador said quiet as a mouse. "Don't worry, you'll **come to see it** all too clearly, one of the terrors of survival. Well? Karen, Julie, Dishcloth?"

More hisses erupted from the daughters, making scratch marks in the air, and meant it. Nickador gave a broad, now typical, smile. They had not evaded his worst nightmares.

"Listen, you barking corpses, anyone of you who gainsays me, but also whoever of you tries to blackmail the other, anyone who spills anything to the authorities, everyone of you here loses everything, including you, Ma." The woman breathed heavily but remained immobile. "Now Pa willed over half his fortune to the good Doctor for his future good works and past ops, he is perfectly aware and thankful for the present situation as he sees it; the rest goes to dear Ma here to divide among you, Karen, Julie... who, with Ma, are also legally bound to be permanently domiciled here in the Grandville family seat, or lose all. The good doctor Klein is the sole Executor."

"Hey, what about me?" Dishcloth protested once too often by far. He was downed with a single hiss and a tiny scratch into a corpse.

Nickador pressed on, "And no snitching, or 'denouncements,' that would mean discovery, early retirement and - poverty." The women quailed at the dreadful word – Nickador had remembered that 'one for all and all for one' was the motto in these hideous chambers of assassins! "Ma and her two lively girls here, signed the agreement to 'assisted suicide', didn't you? You planned it from the start, you were all in it, you and your blessings of Pa, your lobster treats, your death-trap of a car, you two hopeless harpies, Julie and dare I name my own wife, Karen! so far gone in vice she couldn't even pretend to the virtues she never had. To confirm all this, contact the good doctor at his new multi-million Clinic in Tuscany, his Head Nurse, a great witness with a marvellous figure, and faithful wife now, will confirm it! To conclude, and it was me who knew it all, ironically, from a humble Concierge's hideaway. You, you most unnatural girl-devil offsprings perpetrated the death of your own soulless, murderous fucking Pa at your finger-tips!"

"He fucking well deserved it!" broke in Ma, "trying to take what was rightfully mine!"

"Hiding the Will in a bloody pot!" expostulated Karen, " deserves awful punishment!"

"Using all those rosy sex toys!" Julie pretended a sob of disgust.

Nickador grabbed the only bottle of Remy Martin in the room and pressed on, still with that ghost of a special smile the while on his lips, "I intend for the spirit of the good doctor and myself to hang over you all for the rest of your miserable, bloody existences, that is the verdict of this court, to live under eternal suspicion which may be broken at any time, for the rest of your nasty, brutish, short, eviscerated lives. **My bags are ready**. You can all dismiss, I have goodbyes to make and embraces to do." As they turned to leave, Nickador was moved to add as a kind of comforter for them, "You are all so lucky. Look, a free bed for life, - but no sub-letting, mind - three tasty sea-meals a day, you'll all be as one, in the well-appointed homely Grandville nest, side by side, for life, together at last. There's no shame in that, don't worry."

The women flushed, Dishcloth quivered, and all dissolved into the night shadows like the images of silent discarded water-colours of broken clouds in a bin, never to be retrieved, never to be reviewed. Nickador reflected as he raised the bottle of Remy Martin to his lips, but one thing to go –there remained one unanswered point - Pa was already on the road to recovery from the lethal oleander fumes but, at the end of the day, it had been just a simple final battle between Nickador and Pa; as for the antidote overdose, the good doctor and his pleasant Head Nurse had made up the menu to the last hyperdermic and retired to a respectful distance, after all, Nick was a part of the family -more than enough - to administer the last rite. There is no justice, only poetic justice, reflected NIckador, and the Grandville monsters have just had a good dose of it. Status quo is the order of the day, and a pretty punishing one, for a very long time.

Nickador went out onto the balcony. He glugged freely from the bottle, raised his arms to the far shore across the magnificence of the Lake. **Hey, Dr Ash,** curse, bless you now, how are you so miraculously able to view Bad Blossoms from Heaven and Fair Flowers from Hell whenever you like… how do you do it? – you know the two-faced floral tributes in their entirety, the foul buds, widow-prepared for all deceased hubbies: Forget- me-Nots, tons of those, in never-ending sprays; Monkshood, pale and stinky; Oleander, Rhodondendron, all leaves, branches, roots and tubors reeking alright; Star of Bethlehem, especially at sunset; English Yew, everywhere; Baneberry, Fool's Parsley, that caused a laugh now I come to think of it - Meadow Saffron, Moonseed, specks of Ergot on your sleeve; Foxglove thimbles; that I regarded as very funny indeed, because those collections were the lovely petal bundles for us all, daily terminants of last birthdays, hyperdermics even nastier, north, south, east, west, *quietus*, you had to laugh again - the cure was forever, it rubbed all your wrinkles out, till you were smooth as a gravestone. Ha, ha, ha! as you say! So Farewell to Simon and son, farewell to lost Cherrymen, Maurice the Noose, Failures tall and short, bald and hairy , the Bucket and Clearance people , like I, Tan the Tryer, Dominique, his cop mate, Dad the noble, Levitation Man the Seeker, Chitti the Chrystal Maker, Paddy the Guinness, Theodoric Hyacinthus the Crane Spectre, Blondie Defiant and Co, Head Nurses – just, and their Good Doctor Lovers, the Lebanese Six-Shooter, Mr Hughes, the Just-in-time Man, the Saviour,

Dr Papanda the Soother of Youth, Jumpers, Dumpers everywhere, everywhere…. Doctor Ash the Ineffable, the unavoidable, great Trouper of the sky's the limit and permanently present in the lighter side of the human spirit, farewell Ash, mate, never to be pushed aside, never to be overlooked. Thanks for the glimpses, pictures, flashes, memorials, sketches, wind-swept faces, pained expressions, thanks for them all, just trying myself to erect a tiny whisper of lastingness into the absent souls in vacant plots, you'll all make it, never fear, the good always make it. As for the rest of you unmentionables - Harriet the Razor, Tom Gerry and Mike, apprentice Family Slayers, Karen the Faithless as a sow, Julie, Nature's Whore and Nasty Thrush, Dishcloth the Eternal Trailer, the College Director of Thumbscrews, Grandpa the Grisly, Pa the Vice of Life, and Ma the original Incubus, the Gorgon of Existence, now I urge you all to fulfil the destiny laid out for you, you came into life, that cannot be helped, but now prepare yourselves for your exit - which simply is to die and rot like dead rats in a drain, so don't hurry, now, wrongs always putrify in the end, and let your eternal insufferable images of evil, pain and gloom , go with you, - so die, die, die! – at last into the shades with the Eaters of the Dead! and may the most engulfing black avalanches of all bloody time fall upon your shrunken cannibal heads forever!

Nickador picked up his bag and went **to the station**. He jauntily mounted the steps of the carriage, humming, 'twinkle, twinkle little star…' and saluted his travelling companion already in his compartment, yes, Dr Ash himself. They both settled down into the 5.50 intercontinental non-stop express from Geneva direct to Minervia and the rest of the dark and glorious world, for the very last and the very first time too, and no mistake!

Hwyl and Farewell!

SHORT STORIES

MOUNT ERYRI

Emyr hurried towards the hospital in the haze of a hot summer afternoon. The straggling concrete piles of brieze blocks were built on a wide level space at the foot of the hill called 'Mount' Eryri. The whole site was run down, unkempt, unpainted, with faded notices, 'Accident and Emergency,' 'Obstetrics,' etc, barely decipherable – all units neglected to the point of 'unfit for purpose.' Ironically, by contrast, the airy slopes above teemed with the local green and golden fairy rings, buttercups and clover – the playground of the 'Tylwyth Teg,' 'the Fair Folk' - his dear late Mam's abiding belief. The long shadows stretched ahead as he passed the style which led up to the solitary hill-path so beloved of the family. How he missed Mam, how they all missed her. How she had enjoyed this walk with its stone walls, its flocks of sheep, its purple heather, its yellow gorse stretching up among the rocky outcrops, the dull green of the lichen on the boulders and the worn tracks of sheep, hares and rabbits criss-crossing the fields. You could always smell the perfumes of the blossoms in the high breezes, an enchanted place, from where the Fair Folk, according to Mam, played their mischievous pranks on helpless mortals. She knew the Fair Folk were behind 'all things great and small' and it was the Tylwyth Teg's final outrageous jest on her to build this instant modern ruin to spirit her soul away.

But now, was it Dad's turn? Was 'Dad,' known respectfully in the district as 'the Major,' really on his death-bed? Was his son Emyr, their only child, to be deprived of his father as well? Emyr paused at the worn, plywood swing-doors of the Emergency Ward. He could hardly raise a hand, let alone push his way in. Mam had warned him - Yr Arglwydd Angau, the Lord Death, out of Uffern, or 'Hell', was the first to be alerted in any emergency, his ebony sentinels, the body-snatchers of Annwn, waiting for his command at death's door. But never mind, 'trust in the Fair Folk!' that was Mam all over, 'and all dangers will be removed with a 'click' – was she right?

With an effort, Emyr thrust his way into Dad's room, the last one available on the day of his seizure – and froze. His Dad, all fifty-five years of him, lay flat on the iron-frame bed, the yellow and red-stained sheets thrown back, his night-gown sodden with sweat, plastic drips feeding into his forearm in a tangle of tubes. A shaft of sunlight from the small window gave the cell an unexpected warm amber glow. Sam, the head male nurse, was in the act of mopping up blood oozing from the tight line of stitches across his father's belly, fresh dressings ready on a metal tray beside him. The burst ulcer was pumping again. His father, eyes tight shut, began shouting out garbled words of command, all fading to whispers as Sam stroked his fevered brow. Sam possessed the rare gift of reassurance, the aura of which seemed to settle by its own accord over his ministrations and patients. Many of his charges died with a smile on their lips, a gift which was regarded with awe in the community. The Major had been adopted by Sam the moment he had arrived, and Sam had been adopted by the Major as soon as he had regained consciousness.

The Major's voice rose urgently again, " …no!… Sergeant's dead?! Stretcher bearers! Damn!" He imitated the sound of rifle fire, "Crack, crack, crack! Counter attack! Lieutenant Banks! The reserves. Along the ditch! The flares! Zero four-one, same range. Yes, AP, open sights. Red co-ordinates, XI4 G93! Fire!" An agonized shout came from his father, "hell, I'm hit….I'm hit!…" he clutched his chest.

"…OK , Major, just lie still," Sam said. The Major's body relaxed. His voice trailed off.

"Dad!" Emyr pleaded, "It's Emyr."

At the sound of the familiar, loved tones his father's eyes opened and focused on the blurred figure in front of him.

"Emyr! What you doing here?" His voice rose again." I told you. Go! Get out! Can't you see? Your father's dying, you don't want to remember him like this! Go!" his words ended thin as a child's. "Go – please!" he urged. Sam nodded to Emyr. Emyr retreated hesitantly to the corridor, unable to tear his eyes off his Dad. He loved him, the tough kindly old Major, more than any other being in the world. He slumped against the wall. A few minutes later, Sam joined him.

"Is he…?" stammered Emyr.

"…it's easing now…"

"…take my blood," said Emyr, in desperation, holding out his arm.

"Your Pa'll be OK, Emyr."

Emyr nodded dumbly. "You sure?"

Sam gripped him by the shoulder, "Take it easy, man. Think of your Mam…and…"

Emyr recalled his walk to the hospital " … her mountain people," he spoke slowly, " the Fair…Folk…." he finished - and stared at Sam. Sam had the gift. Mam and Dad were right. But would Sam click in time? In a turmoil of grief and a touch of relief, Emyr walked out of the hospital, hands clenched, eyes cast down, moving like a ghost under the shades of Eryri. He stopped briefly to watch the sheep as they cropped the rough grass. They seemed more placid than ever. They kept their eyes firmly fixed on their feed as if nothing else existed. He thought of Mam and her meadow blossoms and the Fair Folk and their elusive other-worldly enchantments and 'glamors' (spells.) Emyr shuffled to a halt. Another click? Emyr groaned again at the image of Dad's bleeding wounds and his battes with old scars. What was happening after all? He stared at the heights of the 'Mount.' For a moment, the Fairy Rings seemed to burn more brightly, the trefoils and buttercups to shine more lightly, and a faint unexpected sense of peace descended over him, followed this time by a feeling of something impending, something momentous - good or evil he had no idea - but imminent and irresistible. Then, 'click' again, and everything faded back to normal, as if Sam had waved a magic hand over the whole scene He glanced around. Had Sam followed him? Was he with him as well? Was it really going to be OK? He gazed at the fields and their spreading slopes laid out like soft green blankets in the sun. Then, click! Again, he heard the summer breezes rustling in the leaves and smelled the sweetness of the gorse. He seemed to see through the wind as it whirled upwards past him towards the jagged summits. Yes, click! he'd had a glimpse! - they really were there, Mam, Dad and Sam, but were they in time?

In his basement hospital lodgings - one room with a toilet - Sam knelt before his makeshift altar, as he did every day. He put on his cape of green and gold and his coronet of blue periwinkles and poured out a libation of melted honey into a baboon's scooped cranium, as his beloved parents had taught him before he fled his native Haiiti. He prayed to the Legba, the High Priests who existed at every cross-roads of life, to suspend all earthly punishments, deserved or not. As a token of his belief, he clasped his hands around the 'cup,' drank the holy libation, spraying the last mouthful over the altar, then bowed and shook the deep-sea life-granting coral shells around his neck. His prayers completed, he ventured out into the afternoon. He had the local Twlwyth Teg to thank again.

Emyr walked along that ancient hospital track for six weeks, day in day out, and every day his father refused to die. Then the bleeding stopped as suddenly as it had started. His Dad's recovery seemed to be on the way at last. After all the agonies and dolours and doubts, Emyr's own self seemed to have been transformed as well – yet not quite. It was as if he had been visited by something life-changing, a blue cloud in a time of peace, which had come out of the future, to envelop the present, to embrace his very existence with an excess of sudden tenderness. Was this joy in himself? Yet he felt bound to ask this new person, how was it really going to work out? Would the Fair Folk let his Dad off the hook, or would the ebony sentinels step in at the last moment with a resounding chop, like the Legba Sam was always warning about. But his Dad's scars were now definitely on the mend although he had to wear a truss every time he got up. Was he safe this time? Was he really OK as Sam had said? Would the stitches split again? Was Emyr's vision of his own new existence the truth or just one of the more cruel delusions of the time of mourning. He was walking to the rendezvous his Dad had arranged with him much earlier, the style at the foot of the mountain. As he gazed upwards, Emyr was convinced this was his Dad's last time on this spot, but that it would be a very long last time. And was there some special event to celebrate first? Or had Mount Eryri and its unseen universal little fabulists already decided the issue?

On the sixth day of the final week, the Major discharged himself, dressed in his old tweeds, got his walking cane, called for Sam and marched off to the meeting point. Emyr waited anxiously. What was his brave, fantastical Pa up to this time? On his arrival, without a word, Dad pointed at the worn track, climbed the style, and set off at an alarming rate, leaping over the stones like a mountain goat, only pausing at the Fairy Rings where he rushed around like a happy child, tearing up bouquets of buttercups and daisies which he scattered over Sam and Emyr. Then it was off again. Emyr and Sam had to push themselves to keep up with him. When they had achieved the highest of the rocky summits, his Dad finally relented, and leant breathlessly on his stick as he gazed at the rolling, fresh, green pastures below. Emyr came up, brimming with questions. Sam, with a knowing smile, seemed to have exhausted his. Had he already paid his dues!? Without a word, Dad turned away and began cantering down the lumpy, tufted gradients, going faster and faster. Emyr shouted for him to stop - his Dad had done enough to flatten a hundred molehills! After the mad strains, and Emyr's shouts, Dad merely speeded up. As they arrived back at the meeting place, Emyr drooped, Sam grinned, the Major paused, felt his bandaged wounds, nodded, then snapped to attention and saluted the whole of the mountain in a single sweeping utterly respectful, gesture, then smiled lovingly and reassuringly at them both.

"Why Dad? Why?" Emyr finally blurted out.

The Major pointed at the Fairy Rings, "Your mother told Sam here and Sam told me, also here, that if I could scale Eryri like a hare and gallop down like a goat, with not a bleeding drop in sight, and finish with a heartfelt 'thank you' to the Fair Folk, I would live here right into my nineties."

And, CLICK! – HE DID!

"WHAT A GLORIOUS PISSOIRE HERE IS BORN!"

God, he needed a pee, and so badly! He clutched his crotch as he lurched down another corridor of the large rambling country mansion. There was bound to be one somewhere here, no amount of cutting grants to ancient monuments could banish the absolute necessity for piss-houses, private and public, with their gleaming sweet-smelling cousins, the toilet bowls. In the passageway, he could hear the wedding guests through the open window. The happy folk perambulated among the adjoining borders and the avenues of climbing roses. And why not? It was a joyous occasion - it was his marriage day! Everything had gone without a hitch - except for this sudden very urgent pain in his lone bladder. Was it the night before? Was he still carrying all those gallons of bachelor pints? No thought of it at the time. But now? He gasped and clutched again. So what was this all about? A punishment? A threat? And if so, over what? All he needed was the relief of one lengthy decent pee and he'd be back to his old self. He glanced ahead. Yes! a short brown door. Bound to be it! He pushed hard and promptly fell into the filthiest toilet he had ever been in. It was also the smallest. A dwarf could hardly have sat on it, let alone shat in it! The ceramic areas of the bowl were smeared with dried shit of the ages. By its side was a stained enamelled receptacle filled with used newspaper. More of the yellowing newsprint was torn in half, and hung from a nail in the wall for the next client. The discarded scraps were smeared with faeces, some obviously, he saw, had been used twice, or more. He fell out backwards, puking, and heaving. Another hygiene nightmare. Typical! They *had* cut back on the allocations for historic properties. A lack of cash had given way to a plethora of shite!

He heard familiar voices coming from the garden below. He looked out of the corridor window and saw his new Pa-in-law and his two fresh-faced brothers-in-law march into the garden space and come to a halt at the border directly below. They about-turned, facing away from the house. They all wore the same hand-made silvery acrylic suits which flashed and shimmered in the sunlight. Pa-in-law had paid for the entire wardrobe of his flashy offspring, no doubt his way of signalling approval of the match. And it was all going so well, except for the bridegroom's sudden dash for the toilet. But surely he had done the poo well enough by now! The Pa raised a hand and the three stood in line like a line of squaddies on parade. As if to drill numbers, they unzipped their flies and in one breathless moment began to piss, hissing into the flat grass. The lawn had recently been mowed and the cuttings lay on the surface in neat rows . He could now hear the rushing and splashing from where he stood. He could also feel an irresistible drop of wee developing on the end of his John T. He came to a rapid decision. In a second he was down the stairs and out to the Pa's sodden space of greensward but his beaming in-laws were already marching off to the Pa's "left right, left right!" Just before they turned back into the side garden, Pa gestured to the steaming place of yellow spillage, and motioned to him, an unmistakable invitation to join in the family baptism and to make his own joyous contribution. He unzipped at once. He would not let his new family down! He noticed the amber trails of his predecessors, an aesthetic touch there! – had formed themselves into three separate perfectly symmetrical circles which stood out among the cut grass, the smallest 'o' directly in the middle. He would show them, the new boy on the block! - he aimed, and his swift flood inundated the cropped greenery. Quelle cascade! Never before had he felt so relieved, never so fulfilled, uplifted even, never had anything been so worth waiting for - and that included visiting some of the earth's foulest toilets! He grunted with satisfaction as he shook off the final beaded bubble and gazed at the glistening tracery of his recent creation. He had not let them down. Yes, he saw his aim had been true, he had indeed hit the bull's eye, the family 'o', and his unique signature was now mingling with theirs. He stretched out his arms over the sacred place and cried out, "Oh, ye fellow shitters of the world, see what a glorious pissoire here is made!"

THE BARON OF BEEF

I'd left the College early that day, fed up with the rowdy dinners, the clattering corridors, the strident students, the tolling bells of universal timetables, and the fucking endless new gadgets of the day. I decided to have a drink before I got home, a rare treat brought on by the common classroom exhaustion and the pupil aversion of the end of term. At least, that was my excuse. I sighed and glanced upwards. There, swinging before my eyes was the pub sign, 'The Baron of Beef.' This dump would do. It was sufficiently anonymous, shabby and empty. I entered the room called 'Saloon' on the ancient frosted bar-door. I approached the counter. No one in sight. The whole place reeked of dry rot and imminent demolition, another decayed watering hole disappearing down the plug-hole of British breweries. I waited and finally rattled a few coins on the counter. A Landlord appeared, bleary eyed from slumber and quite uninterested in his customer. I was about to nod, in a friendly way, when he interposed, "What can I get ya?" "Half of bitter, please." The Lethargic One slowly poured out a glass of piss-coloured liquid. The man's manners were far below my toleration level, while his service quality was off the scale. I decided to leave after the drink, if I could drink it at all. The landlord plonked down the glass and retreated to his sullen cave or private dungeon below stairs. I heard the saloon-bar door click open and shut. I was alone no longer. The stranger joined me at the bar. The Landlord staggered into view again exasperated by the arrival of yet another customer. He served the same ghastly stuff I'd been favoured with, and disappeared without a further grunt. I wondered whether I should address the newcomer, or was he one of the Landlord's moronic tribe? After a sip, he broke the silence, "Beer's not up to much."

"Agreed."

"My first visit here. In fact my first visit to this town. …"

"…you here on business?"

"No idea I'd be here," he said, "I only stopped because I spotted a free parking place and needed a pee."

"I've never been I in here either. I'm a teacher and I don't drink during the day. Holidays soon, thank God!"

"You going anywhere special?"

"Home probably, to relax."

"Best place. We usually go on a farming holiday, you know, put up at a working farmhouse, follow the timetables of the farm, down to the mucking out. We love it."

"Whereabouts do you go?"

"We always go to Wales."

"Really?! Where?

"West Pembs, the national Park, a small farm on the coast, goes down to the sandy beach and the sea." I pause.

"Which part exactly?"

"Near a village called Mathry." I felt a cold tingle going up my neck. "Here, I'll show you." He took out his wallet and extracted a photograph. "There, me, the wife. There, the farmer, his misses, sitting on the bonnet of their old Rover." I was tongue-tied, and not only momentarily.

"What you think?" he finally asked, "great, eh?"

I pointed, "that 'farmer' is my cousin and that is his wife…" The stranger dried up, gaping, "what…?" he stuttered, why… what…?"

"…and you're right, they're sitting on the bonnet of their old Rover. My cousin's name, by the way, is Kenfin Charles and the name of the farm is Glasfryn."

The stranger was now becoming thoroughly disturbed.

"Why…what, does this… I mean…?"

"…it means you can't go on your holiday there this year."

"…we're booked in, it's done. I mean …?"

"…it's saying you can't go there on holiday this or any other year.

"What you mean…!?"

"I attended my cousin Kenfin's funeral last week. That's what it means."

He looked at me again wide-eyed, and sidled off towards the door, a thoroughly mystified and very uneasy being. I watched him as he left, as puzzled as he. The latch rattled for the last time for either of us and the man was gone. The Lethargic One had heard our conversation and had come out to see what the hell was going on. He was in time to observe his customer's departure.

"Well," he said with a shrug of the shoulders, "takes all sorts, I s'ppose…"

THE WAGES OF WEN SIN LO

The night we met, she had removed her wedding ring. Like a prat, I believed she wasn't married - half Belgian, half Chinese, Wen Lo had inherited the striking good looks of both parents. "Hello, my darling!" she had said, embracing me and immediately set to caressing my crotch. Our affair was reaching critical point – she didn't know what to do. We were in her palatial architect's block of offices in the centre of Cambridge. Her private apartment was situated on the ground floor. She handed me a drink, the usual Glenlivet twenty-year old whisky, white as sin!

"Do not worry, I have left him for good this time. It is definite," she assured me. Like many people who have picked up English as a second language, she never used contractions. Still caressing, she complained of her husband again, "he is good looking but stays in bed every morning, just sleeping. I go up here to do work, to earn the bread. He just hangs around. I come back unexpected last week and I find him on the sofa with a bottle, reading a pile of science fiction magazines. I walk out. Now he is coming here soon, to have a final chat, he says, so you will have to go. He says he wants me back, body and soul. He says that, and he is lazy as a mouse.

Do not worry, I know him. He has lost all ambition and does not care I pay for the living. He will not stay long, I promise, I know what he wants. You go, come back in a couple of hours. Go to the park, have a walk, feed the ducks!" I laugh, and that was all, no use trying to understand. This was just it. I had a sneaking sympathy for her poor prick of a husband, but I, one Nickador, myself, wasn't much better - and reading sci-fi mags all day didn't sound too bad an idea either.

"Go now, I will have it sorted by the time you come back, my love."

So, to the park I went, as instructed by my beautiful long-time deceiver, the half Oriental, fully mendacious, babe. I even bought a packet of biscuits along the way to feed the fowls and fishes. On the river bank, the sun shone down on the voracious quacking furry little ducklings who paddled around gobbling their unexpected feasts in the shadow of their ever-caring ma, as if there were no cares in this fucking, ducking, lying world.

On the stroke of two, I made my way back to the apartment. She was waiting in the sitting room, another whisky at the ready. She had the air of a satisfied, replete matron after a banquet, and was in the process of putting on a deliberately enigmatic smile for me, Nickador, her demon lover, - a phony Mona Lisa here, if there ever was one, I noted with a sinking feeling. She squeezed me again and again.

"Well, what happened?"

"He had a knife, he threatened to slash his wrists." She held up her hands. There was no sign of a wound.

"Jesus! are you alright"

"Yes, he missed!" she declared and remained artificially poised, her hands held up as if warding off a blow. Her expression remained firmly and artificially enigmatic. This would convey to him, she felt sure, just how serious she was about their affair.

""Body and soul!" he said to me," she went on, "I want you back, body and soul," again and again, but he has said all that before. He will not try it. He is too lazy and the knife was too blunt. Ha, ha!" her laughter was full of a totally false bravado.

"But what *did* you do?"

"What I always do, gave him a cheque for all the wages and the expenses for our assistants for the last two months. I gave him a drink too!" She said coquettishly. "After a while, I got him to calm down and he left to pay our employees - and buy more sci-fi mags, I suppose. But what did you do?"

"Fed the ducks."

She laughed that laugh again –in sympathy with the ducks or her husband, or himself, he wasn't sure.

"So my darling," she went on with a melting glance, "we are really alone at last." She resumed her pelvic explorations. "Come on," she urged and drew him into the bedroom. He noticed at once that the bedclothes were thrown back, dishevelled as if they'd recently experienced rough usage. When he stripped off and got between the rumpled sheets, he could still feel the warmth of the previous occupants - the wages of Wen Lo, no doubt!

DO IT YOURSELF PARTY

My old school mate, Harry, had invented a new sort of party – an 'après honeymoon bash' he called it. I arrived late at his spacious house to enjoy one of these. The guests were mostly well on the way, as they were expected to be at any party Harry gave. He hurried over to greet me. He looked bronzed and fit. "Hope you had a terrific honeymoon," I said. I couldn't resist it. Harry's eyebrows shot up and down. "Non-stop, you know!" he said, wriggling his pelvis. No one believed Harry would actually marry the girl, Sujatha, an Indian computer graduate from Mumbai university, who had slipped the family bonds, and now enjoyed her new liberty in the West. She had a huge pair if tits, which everybody ogled, a narrow waist, pert bum, and lithesome legs. Tempting enough. I liked what I saw and she knew it. She had but one disadvantage and it was a considerable one, her face. Although well-shaped, it was covered with mini-pustules, all in various stages of disintegration. This was somewhat redeemed by her eyes which held a permanent expression of smouldering sexual desire. We'd had a great first meeting. She now whirled over to me, "Hey, Harry !, I'm going to show Jim our new garden," she sang out and tugged me through the dancing guests, through the French windows and stepped outside, "The new spare loo," she said pointing at a short brick building which I thought was a garden shed. "Just built, part of the extensions!" "How are things going?" I finally ask. She pursed her lips. "I can talk to you. I can tell you. He's no good in bed, just drinks every night and just lies by me, snoring, I didn't know what to do." She shrugged again, sending a shiver of lust through me, "So I have to do it myself, you know, play with myself." She unzips, thrusts her middle finger into her crotch, rubbed it vigorously, took it out, sniffed it, and grabbed me by the arm. "I have to get up and go to toilet here and masturb me, myself, every night. No honeymoon. Come in here." She guided him urgently into the toilet, pulled down her cotton trews and panties, sat on the plastic loo lid and began pleasuring herself. He leaned over her. Her unsightly pimples faded in the darkness. Without further ado, he slipped down his trousers and in a second they were grinding away. It seemed they'd gone on for an hour or more, until she abruptly bent down, covered his cock with kisses, licks and sucks, until he had come, then stood up, and rapidly pulled on her clothes, "he'll be wondering where we've got to," she laughed. They both strolled back to the large sitting room. Harry was standing by the French windows, now quite drunk, "hi, you two," he said with a grin "how's it going?"

"Sorry. Got to go to the little girl's room," Sujatha interrupted, pointing at the toilet. We both watched her walk away, her trews rippling in the breeze. "Shit," mumbled Harry, "what a lay. All night, non-stop, can't get enough. She's just given me the signal, she wants it, and right now, in the toilet there, gives her a kick, my new après honeymoon bash, find your own partners! See you later!"

EVER PRESENT

Mary stood at the breakfast table hastily packing the last of the Xmas presents. "Hurry up," she said to her husband Brian, "We'll be late for Auntie Beryl's party." She paused, "why does everybody always send her a present, even an actual money one sometimes, she's the richest woman in town, the old skinflint. Look at our present from her." She held up an unopened package," a bloody book again, re-wrapped, and not her own purchase either, I can guarantee, it's a present from someone else, 're-cycled,' for the likes of poor bloody us, to save her the expense. Why send her a present, ever? "Why?" you ask. Well, something to do with a possible legacy in her will, no doubt."

"Heck, it's the same every year, nasty old miser."

"Well, why don't you do something about it instead of complaining all the time?"

Brian stood stock still for a moment. "Cash presents," you said!" he exclaimed, giving her a kiss, "that's it! Yes. Yes. Got it! Time to teach that old money-grubber a lesson." He bent down and whispered his plan into her ear. Mary's dawning smile turned into a loud laugh! "

Yes!" she said, "you have got it!"

Half an hour later, they were standing in front of the gorgon herself. Auntie Beryl was seated in the best chair by the fire, her shifty eyes calculating every Xmas gift that was laid on the pile under the family pine tree. Brian nodded to Mary. Mary quietly spoke her recently rehearsed words.

"Some wonderful presents there, Auntie Beryl," Mary pointed at the mound of packages.

"Speak for yourself," snapped Beryl.

"Thank you so much for your wonderful present," said Brian. Auntie Beryl's lips tightened. Young idiot. "No," he protested, it was a really fine and generous present."

"It was only a book," said Beryl, looking sourly at the fool. Mary put in, as arranged. "It wasn't only the book, Auntie, it was the contents *inside* the book." She paused, "You Know."

"No, I don't know."

Mary smiled her sweetest smile.

"What are you on about?" Beryl demanded testily.

"Why, the notes inside the book, Auntie, four fifty-pound notes…" Auntie Beryl's mouth fell open. Everyone in the room heard her gasp of astonishment. She struggled for words. Mary pressed on, "and it so helped us buy presents for everybody, Auntie," said Mary gently. "Thank you from our hearts." She bent down and kissed her now mute Auntie on the cheek, "and a Happy Xmas to you, too."

THE MIRROR OF DYLAN THOMAS
From *Le Sejour des Morts*
by
Jacques Chessex
(tra Dedwydd Jones)

That particular Spring seemed full of snares, especially in the greenwood close to Jean Serre's home. The whole area was criss-crossed with the tracks of the poacher's kids as they set their traps for the rabbits and rodents. Jean decided to take the day off and visit a few of his favourite cafes, not a promising venture for an essentially solitary being.

So in he went anyway to a café in the rue de Bourg in the town centre and sat on the bar stool close to the entrance. He ordered a beer and looked around without taking any real pleasure in his surroundings. There was just a scattering of customers at this time of day with one or two couples whispering in the cushioned cubicles. But he noticed sitting at the far end of the bar a young guy with greying hair, also looking around uncomfortably. He was clearly out of place. English perhaps? He was knocking back his carafe of local white wine, glass by rapid glass, and finished the wine even as Jean watched. He then jerked his thumb at the empty carafe, ordering another. He set about emptying this one with the same gusto and dispatch. Jean was delighted with the scene. This style of drinking appealed to him. Down it went again! The formerly unbending afternoon was making a special offering already. Again! What speed, magnifique! Jesus, this chap is a champion, thought Jean, beginning to forget the miseries of the indifferent world. The second carafe was soon as empty as the first. Again another - ordered with a jerk of the finger. Glass knocked back. Same routine. The guy was slender but well built, not so tall, with reddish hair tipped with gray like a badger's quills. Eureka! And it wasn't as if Jean Serre the writer was particularly hunting for images that afternoon! But it did seem the guy really was wearing a badger's wig, short, thick and silvery at the ends - which gave him a bit of a wild but not in the least drunken, look. But his nose. This was oddly marked at the tip as if a pair of forceps and been strongly clamped onto it at birth and had left its tortured imprint for life. This gave the owner of the nose, in spite of his concentration on drinking, a slightly astonished look, which for some reason, Jean was certain, made him look younger. After the third glass-emptying routine, the guy's eye caught Jean's and his expression became even more astonished. Still gripping his glass, the guy got up, grabbed his carafe and moved across to Jean.

"Hello," he said smiling - with the remnant of an English accent, thought Jean, " I'm fed up. There doesn't seem to exist a living being in this town." He sat down heavily on the stool next to Jean's. Jean was suddenly struck silent, not by the sudden social sortee, but because he had had anther and immediate image – a copse of oak trees, dull under the English rain, with stooped bronzed peasants in leather smocks hurrying to the local thatched pub close by, the Mariners' Arms.

"I'm Welsh," he said, "you know, 'Wales,' it's called 'the south west of England' by the Saxons." Jean understood at once that 'Welsh' for this guy held a vital signifigance. At this point, something stirred in the depths of the recurring image, what was it? Brick-gray sea-banks, yes, running perhaps with the gold and green of sea-lettuce, sea-marigolds in its veins? A weeping willow by a village pond? A sharp-tongued bard's wife, the victim, she suspected, of her master's ancient magic potions? The local mill run by the delightful Miller's daughter, he a bully, she a beauty? Or was that a spinster now, eating her solitary pork chop in twilight in her deserted kitchen, rows of polished copper saucepans behind her, and by the single, small window, a rented TV making more waves than images. Then covering all, the rain in sweeping gusts through the oak trees and salt grass, onwards to the unreachable tides of the endless sea. Through it all, Jean saw that the guy still wore a slightly astonished air.

"So you're sticking with beer are you? Why not?" he abruptly changed his tune although the tone remained the same. "I'm fed up with is country," he went on, "it's beautiful, romantic, the mountain heights, the lakes below, the brilliant vineyards the tidy everything. But I know I can't talk to anyone. The entire populace seem closed in behind invisible prison bars. Would you like to share a glass of this magnificent wine with me?"

"Fine with me," replied Jean. And the barman slid another carafe of white across the bar. The guy filled the two glasses.

"As I said, I'm from Wales, but my wife is Swiss. German Swiss. Shopping with Ma now. I 'm free, making of it as I am able. Very puzzling. People here seem sort of damaged, chipped, you know, like the bits of crockery peasants display in expensive dressers, don't want to talk about it. Well, I do. I want to talk to someone, to learn, you see. I go into a café, loads of folk, but nobody talks! Is there a spell on them? I wrote a play a month ago, I'll send you a copy. At home people talk interminably, the laughs, the quarrels, the adulteries, the spendrifts, who's dying, who's drunk. They're alive, alive! Pity sometimes, but talk about it! Yes, I'm from the land of Dylan Thomas, our greatest poet, and what a voice, what a raconteur!" Jean was at once dumbstruck. Dylan Thomas, his favourite foreign poet! What a life! The guy didn't notice Jean's change of mood, he continued talking, eyes fixed on the distance, vigorously pouring and downing, pouring and downing as if his life depended on it. The next re-play of the original image faded on, filling Jean's inner vision - Swansea, the poet's home town, Laugharne the poet's village, the poetry shed on the sea, empty after his death, smelling of damp, decay and the black dogs of the poet's night. Laugharne again! A herd of pigs running through the tall saline grasses, snuffling and snapping up edibles on every side, chased by beetle-browed village Neanderthals; a tipsy Minister of Religion composing ecstatic hymn tunes, while close by a red-haired parishioner endlessly recited the catechism; the doors of the pub banged to the sound of the distant crashing seas;

above all, the populous darkness, with the strange demented wonderings of uneasy spirits along the craggy cliffs; and in the vanguard of Jean's iresistable reverie, the most vivid of all the recalls, the cemetery of Laugharne itself, with a short white cross placed in the centre with the legend, *'In memoriam. Dylan Thomas R.I.P.'*- Dylan of the spongey country with the hulls of prowling mainlands and bunched copses piled in the soft hills' heel, brimming and bright with poetry for him, the master bard. There, Jean thought, it is all there, the beginning and the end of all voices now caught up in the sound of storms at sea.

"I met Dylan once," the guy announced," I was so young in those days. My father was the local auctioneer, and was granted the sale of all the furniture of Dylan's uncle Harry, of Fern Hill Farm, where Dylan always stayed on his holidays. My old Pa had noticed a small Victorian mirror above the wash basin in Dylan's room, and hung it over my writing table in my own bedroom… good old Dad… yes, I met Dylan once, I met Dylan once…" the guy's voice was low and restrained now, 'I met Dylan once…' as if reciting a prayer for the hundredth time to exorcise some awesome out-of-body experience." "Yes, the mirror of Dylan Thomas, the mirror of Dylan Thomas …' Jean was at once rapt by the incantation. He felt it had taken possession of his soul and would never depart, for the message had risen from the guy's abstracted mouth, as from an ancient spring on St John's Hill and had to be respected.

"So you knew Dylan Thomas," whispered Jean, for some reason feeling he had, in his turn, to repeat the poet's name. At once the image sharpened, and an all-enveloping sense of sadness pervaded his mind. He could see the mirror of Dylan Thomas on the wall. He could make out the very eyes of Dylan, risen inside the mirror, but now losing their sharpness in the mists, giving Jean a last unreachable look from the lost gaze of the poet. Not the end! No! Who was there now, behind the clouds? The Reverend Ely Jenkins and his glorious Odes? No! Dylan again, in his last days, lather on his chin, the razer rasping, nursing fierce hangovers, multiple furious retchings, eyes bathed in alcohol, cheeks flushed, guttural moanings, soft mutterings, head full of horrors, heart full of poetry, Oh, the mirror of Dylan Thomas reflects only but cannot retain the passing apparition of a mortal brother. And why did he, Jean Serre, think of the words of Isiah just then, as if the tragedy of one man was inextricably merged with the quicksilver of another, as in the very pictures of the Mirror of Dylan Thomas?

After that, Jean couldn't quite remember what was said. There was the super wine of course, but also the silences, the unseen dramas of dreams. Then they went their separate ways, but, as vowed over the charged glasses, they did write to each other. Jean Serre received postcards from Wales, of Llanstephan Castle, the estuary of Laugharne, souvenir pictures of the sea waiting for its waves, cormorants and 'the sea-shaken house on a break-neck of rocks;' the play mentioned, *The Drummer*; most striking was an early photo of Dylan, sitting on a tombstone in the midst of the wild greenness of the place, looking sad and sullen, sombre and melancholy, like a small boy punished for a prank he never committed. Dylan seemed sunk up to the waist in stagnant water as if he had been a walker but had been trapped in a pitfall, while behind him a jumbled confusion of graves opened ominously. In this picture, the poet's head is tilted slightly to one side, his right hand plunged into the pocket of his jacket; under the roundness of the face, the laughable funereal black bow-tie like those worn by waiters in his father's day and which he had take up as a badge of his poethood; the Reveren Eli of Bethesda Chapel also wore one, it is said by some, to kingdom come! Now he can see the risen poet passing down Goosegog Lane to Donkey Down, a dozen or so pints at the Mariners's Arms, still moving but unsteady under the paralising poison ivy along the way, staggering, staggering, not advancing, you understand, into the fresh green traps , for the grasping dead of the graveyard were calling him out, enticing him, sucking him down, but no, the poet does not rise to it, his back remains unturned, his half body imprisoned in the wet earth-pit, the buried ones jabber and shriek his name a thousand times to join them, but he ignores them - all this among the vines and chats and reveries of a normal August afternoon!

Jean Serre doesn't visit the bar any more, but every time he passes by, he still hears faint echoes of the would-be dead trespassers from the deeps of the green place. And however briefly, Jean Serre still makes out in a certain mirror, a fixed and dolorous gaze brimming with tears, which living death and deathly life can never wash away. Jean Serre knows this - he has seen it in the mirror of Dylan Thomas!

LETTER TO THE STAGE, MARCH 15th, 2015

The Editor,
Letters to the Editor,
The Stage,
47 Bermondsey St, London SE1 3XT

18 March 2015

Dear Sir,

I shall long remember the March 12[th 2015] issue of The
Stage. It was a revelation in a number of ways. After the
recent spate of stage Awards (The Stage, Jan-March) it
is now abundantly clear that the West End Theatre of
London was won on the playing fields of Eton! Yes,
perhaps, but one must ask - at what price? "A lack of
working class actors" (The Stage 12 March) is one sad
deprivation, with all its glorious clash of class accents
and its rapidly expanding old boy nets. But far more
gruesome things are lurking just beneath the surface
(dramatist Frank Long's letter, March 12th):

The Chastisement of Audiences (by Stoppard) The
Outrage Of Playwrights (by Frank Long)

The Scourge of the Down Dumbers, (more by Long)

The Incredible Shrinking Attention Span (still more by Long)

The Recrudescence of Reminder Lines (by W Shakespeare, and the intrepid Long)

The Wonderful World of Writers' Quotations, (by Billy Sunday, Moss Hart, Kaufman, GB Shaw, Hemingway, and the Bible) all stirred up by the Wrath of the Opera Critics , "There is no more cheap or stale trick in theatre today than 'updating' a classic..." (Rupert Christiansen) The Wistfulness of the Lady-Bird-Girl-Female-Actresses, "Until the average life span is 150 years I do not think that women in their fifties are going to be considered..." (Kristin Scott Thomas.) (All quoted in March 12th issue) and behold, the Untamed Geniuses of Drama, the Directors from Fifty-Thousand Fathoms backed by the Invasion of the Zombie Penguins, are bringing up the unspeakable van, mate, for a very long time.

So, up I say, ye Etonians s and public school chappies and at 'em, ye have nothing to lose but your accents!

Yours faithfully,

DEDWYDD JONES

"There is one, yes, I have one...
The Golden Echo! Spare!
O it is an all youth...beauty-in-the-ghost,
Dearly and dangerously sweet... never fleets more...
O give beauty back, give beauty back, never the least
lash lost...
Where kept? Where -
Yonder. -
High as that?
We follow, now we follow.-
Yonder, yes, yonder yonder,
Yonder."

The Golden Echo (adapted) **Gerard Manley Hopkins**

Lightning Source UK Ltd.
Milton Keynes UK
UKOW06f0718260915

259315UK00001B/1/P